Light and Twilight

To
A.Y.H.
1891-1911

Light and Twilight

Edward Thomas

Laurel Books

This edition first published in Great Britain in 2000
by Laurel Books
282 The Common Holt Wiltshire BA14 6QJ

First published by Duckworth & Co. 1911

Printed by Antony Rowe Ltd
Bumper's Farm, Chippenham, Wiltshire, SN14 6QA

British Library Cataloguing in Publication Data
A catalogue record for this book is available
from the British Library

ISBN 1-873390-03-3

Contents

Foreword	7
THE FLOWER-GATHERER	13
A GROUP OF STATUARY	17
HOME	23
THE STILE	32
THE END OF A DAY	35
THE ISLAND	38
WINTER MUSIC	43
JULY	54
HAWTHORNDEN	63
THE ARTIST	68
BARQUE D'AMOUR	72
OLWEN	76
THE ATTEMPT	80
THE CASTLE OF LOSTORMELLYN	86

Foreword

Edward Thomas stands as a father figure behind several of the leading English poets of our day. His influence continues to grow through his poetry, which is introduced to new readers as an intense, final burst of song cut short by the Great War. After nearly twenty years of literary drudgery, a sketch of his career might say, Thomas found his true and permanent voice reconsidering all that life had meant to him, before laying down his own for his country. Whatever points forward, in his writing and reviewing, to the poems, therefore, is of special interest.

Eleanor Farjeon, when she typed his manuscripts, was the first to see many of Thomas's poems. She later recalled the occasion he gave her a copy of *Light and Twilight*.

'Next morning, I tried to tell him, shyly and inadequately, something of what his writing had made me feel. Then I asked, "Haven't you ever written poetry, Edward?"

"Me?" He uttered a short, self-scornful laugh. "I couldn't write a poem to save my life."'

Thomas's biographers have underlined this sense of a complex development towards poetry and have bound it in with their interpretation of his reaction to the war, and, in the end, his death. He need not have enlisted. He need not have put himself forward to go overseas. He could have avoided the front line. His friendship with Robert Frost and the circumstances of 1914 are judged to have released the poetry latent in Thomas's erudition, critical faculty and a store of obsessively observed experience, laid up over years in notebooks. Before this artistic triumph came the hack work, melancholy, poverty, anxiety and other severe strains on his marriage to Helen.

Walking along with the Edward Thomas who went to war is Another, the country writer, offering in prose a description of what, now, we must imagine. His countryside has gone, for ever, as he may have feared. In one continuous concrete stripe, the motorway now runs from his family's native Wales, over the downs near Swindon, on towards London, penetrating and encircling the landscapes and suburbs of his boyhood. To be distracted by some reminder of the man on the roads he followed is to risk a collision. For anyone saddened by the thought of what has been lost, this is their man.

Somewhere else in the imagination is a place for Edward Thomas the leading critic of modern poetry, carefully reading page after page of new verse before setting down his judgements in clear, suggestive, sparely technical language. Which of these characters can we expect to meet in the pages of *Light and Twilight*?

This is a book of considerable biographical interest, containing acknowledged accounts of important moments, such as Thomas's courtship and suicide attempt, among a number of examples. About half the stories touch on Welsh themes and his Celtic heritage. But these many, clear connections disappoint an attempt to invert the text into a biography, unless, and it is not hard, we persuade ourselves that the death struggle between language and feeling is indeed the story of Thomas's life.

Light and Twilight contains its share of rural evocations, as we would expect. In the opening story, a flowered meadow, that set piece of contemporary 'English' garden design and agricultural anachronism, is given the full treatment. But, to elude our expectations, the next tale brings us to the inner city and takes an unflinching look at the yellow flesh of a starving pauper.

Unlike some of his commissioned works, this book does not hit a crisis of motivation and drag on to die at the prescribed minimum number of words. The last story is one of his finest. The pieces, mostly written for periodicals in the burst of creativity Thomas experienced around 1909, appear selected out of a larger stock for their unity and contrasts. They inform each other of their common themes, which are the moment of death, the spark of love and the patterns of living which these eternities force us to describe. Thomas treats his obsessional subject matter without violence of either phrase or diction and with every intention of delivering the final statement.

His dedication of the book to a young person, dead at twenty, sets the tone for what follows. Margaret, in 'July', dies at the very same age. Of this story, its writer said that it was a mixture of experience and invention which proved him no artist, in a typically provocative, self-scornful aside.

At all times Thomas took great pains to avoid carelessness. He tried faithfully to check that what he wrote he truly meant and troubled himself not to express more than he felt he knew. Despite this restraint, behind the descriptions and actions in these stories move the shadows of unexpressed feelings, shot through by flashes from an experience of transcendence. The reader is being invited to treat each story as a meditation and in the search for a similar awareness, to take Edward Thomas as a guide. Who better? Wonderfully, Thomas does not try to spell out an intellectualised meaning from these moments, only to affirm that they happen. Maybe such meanings held nothing for him.

Light and Twilight displays an exceptionally refined use of language. This is literature. Irrelevant to conjectures about Thomas's personality, here are words joined together with an affinity shown for each one and as established between neighbours. Whether capable of being called poetry or not, which is a question, this is craftsmanship of a high order and the product of a special talent and great application.

There are elements in these stories which merit lengthy discussion and more than space here allows. In particular, the problem aspects of Thomas's mentality as it reflects the climate of ideas just before the First World War. Such topics include the idealisation of women, the use of myth and his susceptibility to a concept of national consciousness. The changes brought about by the cataclysm of that war make it harder for us to hear in the more measured voices from the preceding age precisely what is being said on these matters. However, it can be agreed that writers as serious as Thomas were applying the spade to new ground, to explore what might be called the primitive aspect in human character, in prose as in other arts.

Edward Garnett, a friend of Thomas, encouraged him to publish this book. Some years later, Garnett submitted his friend's entry in the Dictionary of National Biography. He said there:

"The little group of imaginative masterpieces, such as 'Home', 'July', 'The Flower Gatherer', 'Olwen', 'A Group of Statuary' in . . . *Light and Twilight* excel by clear beauty of imagery, grace of contour and delicate, limpid English. 'Celtic magic' and a sensitive freshness and contemplative charm inspire these idylls . . ."

It is difficult to add to this sad tribute. Perhaps we could speculate that another Edward Thomas is to be found in these stories, a man with a complementary identity to the poet who died at Arras and someone with intentions of his own in this category of prose. A half-seen possibility, maybe, but one worth exploring and enough reason to bring this special book out into the day, as a whole, for the enjoyment of new readers and new writers, and the many who have admired Edward Thomas, the artist, through the years.

Patrick Ingram
8th April 2000

Note

The text of this edition is based on the 1911 text published by Duckworth with minor changes to correct obvious printer's errors. Excepting *Winter Music* the stories were first published in *The English Review*, *The Nation*, *The Saturday Review*, *The Nationalist* and *The Thrush*.

Further Reading

The following short list concentrates on accessible editions.

Works

The Collected Poems of Edward Thomas, ed R. George Thomas, Oxford 1981

A Literary Pilgrim in England, Oxford 1980

The Icknield Way, Wildwood House 1980

The Heart of England, Oxford 1982

The South Country, intro. John Wain, Hutchinson 1984

A Pilgrim and Other Tales, intro. R. George Thomas, Dent 1991

Memoirs

Helen Thomas, *Under Storm's Wing*, Carcanet 1988

Eleanor Farjeon, *Edward Thomas, The Last Four Years*, Sutton Publishing 1997

Biography

Jan Marsh, *Edward Thomas: A Poet for his Country*, Paul Elek 1978

R. George Thomas, *Edward Thomas, A Portrait*, Oxford 1985

Critical Studies

Edna Longley, *A Language Not To Be Betrayed*, Carcanet 1981

Stan Smith, *Edward Thomas*, Faber 1986

The Art of Edward Thomas, ed. Jonathan Barker, Poetry Wales Press 1987

Andrew Motion, *The Poems of Edward Thomas*, Hogarth Press 1991

Edward Thomas Fellowship
Membership Secretary, 50 New Odiham Road,
Alton, Hampshire, GU34 1QG

The Flower-Gatherer
"Herself a fairer flower." — MILTON.

So strong was the young beauty of the year, it might have seemed at its height were it not that each day it grew stronger. The new day excelled the one that was past, only to be outshone by the next. Day after day the sun poured out a great light and heat and joy over the earth and the delicately clouded sky. The south wind flowed in a river straight from the sun itself, and divided the fresh leaves with never-ceasing noise of amorous and joyful motion. So mighty was the sun that the miles of pale new foliage shimmered mistily like snow, yet each leaf was cool and moist with youth, and the voices of the birds creeping and fluttering among the branches were as the souls of that coolness and moistness and youth. If one moment the myriad forms of life, and happiness intoxicated the delighted senses, at another a glimpse of the broad mild land stretched out below, and of the sun ruling it in the blue above, gave also a calm and a celestial dignity and simplicity to the whole. One after another the pools, the rivers and rivulets, the windows or glass roofs of the vale, caught the sun and sparkled as if Vega and Gemma and Arcturus and Sirius and Aldebaran and Algol had fallen among the meadows and woods.

On some days the sense of oneness, of wide power and splendour uniting earth and sky, of infinite simplicity, triumphed. On others the spirit was content to bathe and half lose itself in numbers, exuberance, complexity, in the odours and colours and forms, one by one, in the rich rising flood of the grass, in the hurrying to and fro of preparation that was nevertheless not over much troubled about the end.

The children seemed to be trying to gather all the flowers. It was their way of striving to grasp the infinite. They were scattered over the hillside, where the pale sward was made an airy or liquid substance by the innumerable cowslips nodding upon its surface, as upon a lake, that held their small shadows each quite clear. All day they gathered flowers, and threw them away, and gathered more, and still there were no less. The earth continued to murmur with blissful ease, as if, like the wandering humble bee, it were drowsed with the warmth and the abundance.

One child separated herself from the rest, moving down instead of across or up the hill. Often she went on her knees among the flowers, with bent eyes that saw only the hundreds close at hand. But from time to time she raised her head, her delicately browned and yet more rosy face, her gleamy hair, that was as pale as barley on her temples but elsewhere golden brown as wheat, her round and calm yet lively eyes, her restless happy lips — and looked steadily for a moment at the whole of earth and sky, and grew solemn, only to return to the other pleasure of the hundred cowslips just at her feet, the crystal and emerald wings among them, the pearly snails, the daisies and the chips of chalk like daisies. Tighter grew her hand round the swelling bunch. She slipped; the flowers fell and not all were picked up again; and so there was yet room for bluebells when she reached the wood below. In the moister fields still lower there were kingcups of gold and cuckoo flowers pink and white, looking as if they had fluttered down from the sky; and for these also a place had to be found. The stitchworts of a hedge side lured and piloted her to the hollow, hardly larger than a great hall, where a brook ran straight, for once in its life.

By the slow stream forget-me-nots made a continuous haze on either bank. She was now quite alone, under the old cherry tree of the forsaken garden at the water's edge. Six or eight huge crooked branches rising out of the rocky trunk bore up a dome that was all flowers. They were in rounded clusters as of bubbling snow, and close as honeycomb. The lovely freckled white smelt bitter and sweet at once. The flowers hummed with bees, and between the clusters were streaks and wedges of the blue. The child looked up suddenly at this glorious roof, and her smile of surprise passed into what would have been indifference, because the blossoms were inaccessible, if she had not caught sight of the forget-me-nots when the flight of a cuckoo that had been calling out of the cherry-tree carried her eyes away to where he skimmed the water. He did not fly far, nor cease to call while he was flying, or when he was seated on one of the alders by the brook. She looked at him as she was plucking the forget-me-nots. This narrow hollow was his room she thought. Yet it was full of other songs. There were blackbirds hidden in the hazels, or clearly defined against the may flower or the bronzed flowering oaks. Thrushes talked and called out to her a hundred times: "Did she do it? Did she do it? Did she? Did she? She did, she did!" and she laughed. A swallow flew over his image in the water as if about to dive in after it, and then rose up and curved away. Smaller unfamiliar birds sang rillets and minute cascades of hurrying song. The goldcrest repeated a tune like the unwinding of a tiny sweetly-creaking winch, like the well-winch at home. But the lazy cuckoo was lord of all.

Now she had filled both hands, and each time she grasped a new stalk some of the old fell out. So presently she laid them down in the grass to rearrange them. But she now noticed the tall sedges of the brook and wanted some. She looked round to see if anyone could see her doing this forbidden thing, and then went to the edge and stretched out her hand: they were too far. The water was gliding under her, flashing like brandished steel, and yet as clear as air over the green stars of its bed. Everything had always been kind to her, and this water was one of the kindest, so playful and bright, so pure that sometimes they came far to fetch some of it in a pail for the house. She leaned out, and even moved one foot as if to step towards the green sedge. She lost her footing and fell, not quite reaching the blades as she splashed. She was scolded for getting wet, but never much, and she used to laugh as they were dressing her in fresh clothes; and to-day it was so warm. It was an adventure. But her hair was all wet; she did not like that: and the water, though so pure, was not pleasant in mouth, nostrils, eyes, and ears, nor could she get rid of it. Her hands touched the green stars; she could see them; but the sky was gone. She was surprised, indignant, anxious to be out. Why this cruelty? It was not a game to go on like this. She was angry . . . terrified . . . numbed. She could see nothing but water, she heard, smelt, breathed, tasted, touched water everywhere. Who could have done it? Something is cruel ! . . . Why? . . . See could not bear it. No! No! Where were her flowers? Where was her mother?

She rose up a little, and saw the sun, and the cuckoo on the branch through the waves, and heard the man calling to his horses in the next field. Then solitude: all pleasure gone, love, light, warmth, movement was nothing, was over there, was past, or never had been, would never be again. It was better now. Sleep, sleep. But in the sleep, songs, visions of the house, forms and faces moving to and fro, and herself going in and out amongst them, far away, long ago, over there, in that other place. She was hurrying faster and faster, running too fast for her legs, carried away off them into the air, but swaying and rising easily and more easily now. She sighed as she seemed to float higher and lighter into soft darkness, into utter darkness, into nothing at all, where there was never anything or will be anything. The mud settled down. The stream flowed clear and sweet. The sun had not so much to do but that he could wilt the flowers lying on the bank. Life went on exuberant, joyous, august, looking neither to the right nor to the left. The cuckoo called. The birds' songs became so drowsy that they were not missed when they ceased, and only its own echo replied to the cuckoo. The child's white forehead was just above the water, and a fly perched on it and preened his diamond wings. A quarter of a mile away the dinner bell at home was swung merrily again and again by a strong arm that enjoyed the task.

A Group of Statuary

I HAD walked several miles through streets whose high, flat-fronted buildings made me feel as if I were at the bottom of a well, or in a deep, weedy river-bed with cliffy banks, from which it was impossible to climb out, though I could turn aside into many tributaries even more narrow and as deep. The sky was stagnant and dull; the fever and heat of the air came not so much from the sun as from underground, and from the walls on either side — a volcanic fire out of the earth's depths and the hearts of men. The plaited streams of men and women were restless. Their bodies were glad of the heat, but the gladness was repressed, and could show itself only in a darkly burning eye, a caged smile, a beautiful contrast of colours, a restlessness that knew not its own cause, far less a means of satisfying itself. They thought of the country, of the sea, of leisure, of resting on the grass, of sleep, of dreaming, of love; of everything which the prison made impossible, or of nothing at all, merely undulating with the waves of vague desire and discontent. Thousands of faces and figures passing me by were full of capacities, of strength and love. They were like weapons, swords, spears, axes and daggers, slender scimitars and curious twisted edges, hanging on the walls of a museum. They had the same look of being unnatural and out of place as objects in a museum. If only they were to begin taking them down, trying their edges, brandishing them!

One such street led me at last out into a wide pool. A score of streets opened into it, yet it was broad and almost empty. It was dotted with islands where people could take refuge from the stream; only there was no stream; and the islands also were empty. It was a grey flat space, surrounded by many-windowed buildings of a grey that was almost black, a chapel, a factory, a school, public-houses, at the several corners, and all of this same hue. It was shapeless, like a natural pool. It was far larger than the largest cathedral in the world, and it allowed a view of the sky, both overhead, and on every side above the roofs and between the walls of the streets running into it. The islands were girt by low, thick posts. On some there were pillars surmounted by lamps. They were wonderfully silent and still, as if detached in some way from the conditions of the surrounding world.

The largest of the islands, lying at one corner of the pool, was shaded by three plane trees; or rather, being trees, and retaining a few colourless, dusty leaves, they suggested the thought of shade. At first sight, the trees, the emptiness, the space, the quiet, gave the place a rustic or cloistral air as of a cathedral or market town; bullocks in rows, sheep and pigs, crates of geese, farmers going slowly to and fro would have been in keeping with it — or a priest walking at ease with a fine lady. But under the trees there were seats without backs, and the flagged pavement was irregularly worn into many hollows, and plastered with dust and moisture in blotches. On the seats were figures which few could have had difficulty in recognising at a short distance as those of human beings no longer young. It was they who spread round about them the silence which possessed the islands.

Even more fitting than a market or ecclesiastical group was this assembly under the planes. For like a market group, in a market square, it had a look of entire fitness as if it could not have been changed, as if it had been there from the beginning. The dull, grey figures might have risen up out of the city soil, with some of it still clinging to them, rude and shaggy after the effort of birth, to sun themselves and look about. Their greyness was wintry, the rasping greyness of north-east wind that turns dry roads, asphalt, flagstone, plough-land, and meadow in the country, within the mind, to one grey, the colour of ashes. Nothing in them responded to the heat out of the sky. They were of the dark earth.

Before the discovery that they had faces with eyes and lips and hair, it might have been seen that they were men and women, and that for two reasons: first, they wore clothes which subtly suggested those of the people in the crowd, without in the least resembling them; second, they were miserable. I think that the clothes alone, the misfits and cast-offs of scarecrows, would have betrayed them, but I am not sure; I cannot separate the clothes from them, and not them or their clothes from misery. By a swift intuition the spirit penetrated those recumbent or propped-up frameworks of old black clothing, and divined their humanity — penetrated the clothing straight to the spirit, without thinking of the flesh. For in these abjects, as in the sumptuously apparelled, there is something terrible about the mere naked flesh, and it needs the inhuman ironist to think of it with serenity. Of all those who, full of meat and hope, or one of its equivalents, passed by that island, and turned an eye for a vacant second upon those under the planes, not one failed to recognise that these were of one species with themselves. Not one got so far beyond that profound truism as to think of them and to see them naked, merely human, in their approximation to the appearance of a child bathing, a beloved woman a-dream on a summer morning, or a quoit-thrower poised. Had anyone so beheld them he would have stood thinking half the day over it, or he would have run away and stopped his eyes against the siren-sphinx. I saw neither the thinker nor the fugitive.

For all of us it was the clothing that had a meaning, the clothing of other men and other women. The clothes were the human things. The clothes held them together and made them the men and women they were, and these upon the benches had a look as if they would have crumbled away had they been divested of their rags. The body beneath was unconsciously known and feared as something diabolical or divine. The Master Sculptor had wrought them daily throughout a lifetime, and somebody had always come to their rescue on the day when the drapery had seemed no longer to perform its part sufficiently. One man, it is true, lay half along a seat with his head and shoulders in the lap of a woman whose head had fallen forward so as to hide his face with her hair, and his trouser leg had rolled up and disclosed a yellow bone. But the chances of ordinary life do frequently bring to sight a man's bare arm, breast, or foot, though usually it is whitish and something more than bone. This was a yellow bone. Still, it might pass. There was nothing here to outrage those who were not only full-fed but rightly and confidently expecting to remain so. Had it been a woman . . . Apparently there are always enough black stockings left in the poor world to cover the yellow bones of the distressed mothers, sisters, wives, casual mistresses, and daughters of Englishmen; if not a loaf, yet a black stocking. There were men and women lying — men and women doubled up as the cavemen used to sleep and die — men and women with folded arms, and faces looking down or straight over the grey pool at nothing — on the warm seats under the planes. There was not an attitude that could not be equalled among birds on a frosty branch, and, for all that it was not designed for them, their clothing was like a natural covering of plumage or fur, but mangy and soiled.

One of the women was doing up her dusty hair. She had laid her black bonnet on her knees, and her locks fell to the pavement as she drooped her head to one side and combed them with her fingers, her eyelids closed, for there was no mirror. It was a touch of nature. The gesture is always pensively beautiful, and could never fail to remind one of his mother when he was yet a child, and another of his young wife — but there was nobody near, neither were there any windows or private houses looking that way. No one of them spoke, or wept, or sighed. The woman who was doing up her hair coughed now and then. The man with his head in a woman's lap turned over once to spit — he was wide awake. As he once more made his head comfortable the woman revealed her eyes. There was nothing else of her save rags, and the eyes seemed hardly to belong to her. They expressed no private grief or hope or fear, any more than do the eyes in the portraits of Christ. It was a jest of gamesome providence to light those lamps in her face unknown to her, a jest like that of a small boy who chalks another's back. She bore about with her those beautiful brown eyes, and, save that no doubt men would kiss her for them, they served no purpose which is not served by the eyes of a weasel or crow. In a musician, now, in a lovely woman living among mountain lakes — such eyes would have done many missions for the soul. They were like wild-voiced nightingales in their silence. But in this cage . . . Had they really belonged to her, it was inconceivable that she should have been content to sit in that dusty retreat under the planes. A musician or a poet with such eyes would have told us subtle, remote, lustrous things, and, if we had not listened in his lifetime, yet, when he was dead and known to all, his eyes would still be remembered. A passer-by, seeing these eyes, would have been startled, but would have controlled himself by reflecting that they could be matched in a cow's or Irish terrier's, and he would have gone on to remember even with amusement what very foolish people have glorious eyes; it is the inner eye and the soul that count; indeed, what better proof of this could be given than this vision on the bench in the dusty heart of the city, in a corner where refuse had been swept up and left to lie, as by a careless housemaid, because nobody would notice it in such an out-of-the-way place. A girl passing dropped a paper bag opposite to the woman with the eyes, and they saw it. She raised the man's head in her hands, and looking to learn if any of the others had seen, let his head down on the bench. She rose and walked to the bag. First she put her foot gently upon it to make sure that she was right in thinking that it was not paper alone. She was right. She picked it up, thrust in her hand, filled her mouth with something, and putting the bag in her pocket, returned to her seat. Since she saw nothing more that was unfamiliar, or in any way new or worth attention, nothing which she could not see as well without them, she closed her eyes.

All were now still. They absorbed the dry, dull heat.

The pool and its islands appeared to be empty. For no one notices the statuary of London unless it is made for display or to divide the traffic, not to form a decoration appropriate to a particular site, as in the case of these figures under the planes. In all the city there was no group so perfectly in keeping with its greatness and aridity. I had seen equestrian figures, symbolic groups, nudes, semi-nudes, figures in frock coats, in stone or bronze; thousands of living creatures, joyous or beautiful or tragic in their capacity for joy, in harmony with the burning sun, yet having nothing to do with this city which was the work of the giants, the heaven-besieging giants, not the gods. But these thirteen or fourteen recumbent, leaning, seated, and bowed figures, in their dignified dismay, forming neither a circle nor a square, but a group as of a herd or flock were in their place, thoroughly native, children of the city clay — fit lords of the scene, if they had but known — perfect citizens of no mean city. Why should it trouble to house Grecian marbles when it had these eternal ones wrought with its own hands? Could they have been petrified at that moment, and duly proclaimed as the costly work of the most famous living sculptor, none would have denied their pre-eminence. One by one the alien transitory crowd in the surrounding streets, after venturing up to glance at the wondrous art, would have slunk away and have left the city in their possession as theirs by right and theirs only.

It was very still. The sun in the sky was the one thing that moved. I dreamed that this exodus had taken place. I was a traveller in a desert city whose sons had all been dead thousands of years, but were known still to the stranger by these mighty marbles among which the planes had taken root. The tradition of the dead race was so powerful that not a bird or beast or any wild thing cared to visit this memorial of it, except curious men. And I was a man. I consulted the learned authorities and found them divided between two theories. One was that it was a group of that ancient people preserved in their natural attitudes, "while the flesh was yet between their teeth, ere it was chewed" by a petrifying plague. The other was that these were their gods, whose uncouth names I was not skilled to interpret. It seemed to me that the second theory was the better of the two, and, except Stonehenge, I had seen nothing approaching its sublimity in my wanderings.

Home

A LITTLE square sitting room, not very high, and hardly wider than it was high, yellow-lit by a brass lamp in the centre, and shutting out the visible world by three walls of a pleasant dull gold and indistinguishable pattern, and by three narrow curtains of a ruddiness that was dreamily heavy and sombre. On the walls, five pictures at the same height above the tops of the dark chairs, the mantelpiece and the sideboard; and on one, three shelves of books. A very still, silent room; and in it, motionless as in amber, a man standing before the books, and a woman with raised eyebrows and stiff but unquiet hands, dovetailed together, staring into the black-crusted fire. The man, chin on one hand, elbow on the other, tall and upright and dark like a pinnacle of black rock, looking sternly out of kind eyes at the books as at children. The woman, trying to drowse herself through her eyes by the fire and through every pore of her body by the silentness, yet aware all the time of the husband between her and the windows, as though his shadow blackened her instead of half the books. These two, separate and careful not to look at one another. Had they been utterly alone they would hardly have looked thus. They were not alone. In the stillness and silence, despite the walls and curtains, there was another presence, and a greater than they. It was London, a presence as mighty as winter, though as invisible. Its face was pressed up against the window; its spirit was within. And there was yet another, almost invisible, and as frail as the other was mighty — the spirit of the one who saw the room and felt the enchantment of London upon it. Neither the man nor the woman knew what was this second spirit in their room, yet the room was its home. It was the spirit of a young soldier dying in a far land. He was calm and easy now, without pain and without motion. Only his dark eyes told that he lived. As still was he, with bright fixed eyes, as a bird sitting on its nest. One had just left him who had spoken a few words intended to comfort him; but all the words had faded as soon as spoken, just as wavelets on a burning sand which they do not even stain, all except "for your country." He had heard these before without considering them, though he would have struck the man who mocked at them. This time they remained because they instantly recalled the first time he had heard them used, eighteen years before. His father had said to him one morning, "Johnny, I am going to take you to see your country, to-morrow." His pale mother had smiled her patient, weary smile — with some gentle ridicule added — at these words. Then she looked admiringly at her husband, the big, gaunt wry-faced man, whose eyes laughed so under his black brows. She had no country. She was born in the great city where they lived, where Johnny was born, and she had never left it. Nearly everything outside her home inspired her with wonder, awe, or fear, and she held her husband in awe because he had a country of which he frequently talked, where they spoke a different language, had queer names, different food, different ways and, as she dimly conjectured, a kind of common life as of one big family. Her husband had told her often that he had only to take a train to his country and get out at any station over the border, and somebody most likely a cousin, would step up as if he had been waiting, and say, with his face all cut up by a smile, "And how are you David John this long time?" But somehow he never went until this April. He had had to be content with talking, with taking the boy on his lap and singing the songs of his country, grand wailing songs that would often make him happy for the rest of the evening, merry, quick songs that made him tap the ground with his toes and yet brought tears into his eyes, so that he set the child down and went out into the street and came home, bitterly, hours afterwards to the dark house and the meek waiting wife.

But now he was really going to his country. "To-morrow," he said, "we will take the train at midnight, and before noon we will be finding a curlew's nest on the moor just by where the old battle was."

"What battle, father?" said the boy.

"Why, one of the old battles when we beat the English, I suppose," said he.

"But what was the name of it and when was it fought?"

"Ah, I cannot tell you that now: it is not in the history books. But the river there is called the River with the Red Voice, and there is a battle mound. The air is so clean there that a collar lasts you a fortnight."

"Dear me," said his mother, waking with a start from her musing.

Then the boy fell a-dreaming about his father picking up mottled eggs among dead men's bones by a river that ran red with blood.

Those bright eyes in the hospital tent saw now the railway station like a huge palace, sprinkled with lights and paved with multitudes of men and women, and good silent trains stretched out among them which the people had caught by a hundred handles and were mounting, to persuade them to carry them far off into the black night beyond, the unmapped black night with its timorous lines of small lights. He and his father entered the multitude and crept in and out alongside the train; and it was very wonderful, but many of the groups who talked were talking in the tongue in which his father used to sing, and he looked up at their pallid faces and black hair and agitated smiles and boldly moving lips, and was inclined to be afraid, but remembering that they were his father's people he was not afraid, but filled with wonder and admiration. Even some very little children, smaller than himself, were chattering in that same tongue quite easily; it seemed to Johnny that they were very clever little children. How kind everybody looked now! He had never seen so many people smiling and talking friendly before.

"Where is our country now?" said Johnny, and as soon as he had sat down with his face towards the land of his desire, the train was gliding out past a hedge of white faces and white lifted hands into the darkness.

The carriage was full, and the boy liked pressing up against his countrymen on both sides and touching their boots with his toes, and watching the thoughts on their faces and the books and papers they were reading, and how they would sometimes let their books and their papers fall on their laps, and look out at the wild-starred night seriously as if, perhaps, "it had come . . . their country." In a corner opposite sat a young woman, and next her a young man. He was reading. She was doing nothing but thinking, with her eyes turned towards Johnny. Soon the man closed his eyes; his head sank upon the woman's shoulder, but she did not move, only took away the book lest it should fall, and she offered

Johnny a sweet, but he was too busy looking at her, and would not take it. The young woman's brown eyes fixed on him softly, and, his father's arm round him, he began to dream; and he awoke, surprised that he had been asleep, at a cold glittering station with a few faces staring in from the platform, looking for seats. "Is this — ?" He was going to ask his father if they had arrived, but he saw the name of a well-known town on the seats and lamps and again closed his eyes; the others also had looked and immediately closed their eyes. Then nothing — tiny lamps in the darkness — nothing again — then over a hill a large moon began to light a watery sky, black cloud and blacker earth, and looked afraid of the huge world over which she reigned. Another stop, a well-known name on the lamps, and then sleep to the sound of the train expressing steadiness, determination, and content in its rhythm and hope in its speed. If he opened his sleepy lids he saw the young woman's soft eyes, and the earth now grey and not black, and the moon high, without a cloud around or below, with groups of houses lost — as it seemed — in the night and cowering under the trees, here and there a light burning where someone, perhaps, was enviously watching the train on its march of discovery and conquest; or, still later, a pale sky lit from below and behind, as well as from the now invisible moon above, a river gleaming, a horse knee-deep in white mist looking up at the train, a church upon a hill that seemed awake but alone, small contemptible stations where they did not stop.

The fixed bright eyes in the bed saw these stations again in their dreariness, and saddened with the dream that he now was upon such a station, and the lighted train was rushing by and forgetting him, with its proud freight of living men looking ahead towards their country.

Nodding awake again, he saw the girl eating an orange, a wide water like a sea and the pale moon shrivelled beyond it, a farm and its cattle streaming out under a hill covered with crooked oaks, and the cattle were bowed under the weight of their long horns. "It is near," whispered his father: he slept.

When he awoke he was upon his father's knee, and both with cheeks together were looking, over frosty meadows and blown trees, at sand hills and sea beyond, and on the other side at hills crimsoned with bracken, their summits invisible, so steep were they. "This is it," said the father. "Yes," whispered the son, and both looked through and beyond the mountains and the sea to their country, the country of their souls, so that the child's first thought — that this was not what he had expected — never appeared again, until now in the tent. When a gap in the near hill showed them greater giants beyond that appeared to have descended out of the sky, and only half descended as yet, for their crests were in the clouds, the two were not more moved; they could see, far beyond these distances, greater hills, a land even more free.

They stopped, and there were wizard faces waiting, and the strange tongue that was the boy's own was spoken, and they seemed to welcome him. He began to step down from his father's knee to get out — but no, not yet.

They stopped again where there was only a black-bearded, tall man and a sheep-dog waiting. They could hear the thrushes sing, under the clear blue and the lightless moon, from out of dark thickets in a hollow rushy, land, backed by the sea and the orange sails of vessels that caught the dawn. "Over there," said his father, pointing beyond the ships, "is the land we have come from." It was as faint and grey and incredible in the distance as his own land was clear and true; and he sighed with happiness and security, and also with anticipation of the further deeps that were to be revealed, the battlefield, the curlew's eggs, the castles, the harps, the harpers harping all the songs of his father. He had got so used to the faces of the men, which were like his father's, that when his father asked him whether they were not different from the English, he said "No," and was scolded for it.

The sun and the bright world dazzled his eyes. He slept. Then, a black barren land, a host of tall black chimneys between hills and sea, fountains of black smoke, sheaves of scarlet flame, red-hot caves . . . Young men crowded into the carriage and burst out into a song. It was in the language that Johnny spoke, but the beauty of their voices in harmony made it different from anything he had heard before that day.

A marsh and a thousand sheep, gaunt hills on one side, sea on the other, and the young men singing a war march in their own tongue at his father's request. It made him afraid at first. Then he fancied that the battlefield was not far off, and they were going to it, and the song was sung to hearten a host of which he was one. He felt grim, but glad and bold as he looked at the dark young men and thought of "his country."

"My country," muttered the dreamer lying still, and blinked his eyes as the tent flapped and he saw outside the sun of another country blazing and terrible as a lion above the tawny hills. The country that he had been fighting for was not this solitude of the marsh, the mountains beyond, the farms nestling in the beards of the mountains, the brooks and the great water, the land of his father and of his father's fathers, of those who sang the same songs, the young men and the old, and the women who had looked kindly on him. Where were those young men scattered? Where had their war march on that April morning led them?

A grim, black-bearded face was bending over him, with smiles deeply entrenched all over it. He was lifted straight into a cart behind a chestnut pony with his father and the man.

The sun was hot. They climbed up high among the hedgeless and pathless mountain, always up. The larks sang. The mountain lambs skipped before the cart.

They alighted by a solitary cottage under the road, whence a maid brought ale for the men and milk for the boy. They sat down among gorse bushes and ate apple tart and cheese, wafers of oat and currant cakes. The men talked. Johnny wandered up from the road with a girl of the cottage. And there with the rough strange mountain boys they set fire to the gorse and dead bracken. The flames leapt up like the genii out of the imprisoning jar in the Arabian tales, and he drew back. The earth was crowded with little flickering plants of fire spreading this way and that. Huge whirls and rounds of the yellow-white smoke soared up against the milky sky. The smell of the smoke heated by fire and sun was delicious. When the earth was black they moved on, while some sent the grey boulders galloping downward till they bounded over the road with a hero leap, and struck sparks out of other boulders or plunged into the gorse. The boys roared, the girls shrieked. All disappeared. But all day they could see the smoke of one conflagration pouring upwards before the wind in a great river, lost awhile in the hollows, seen again continually surging towards the high crests mile after mile, like a gigantic engine smoking wildly over the wilds.

Outside one cottage there stood a little old man, naked to the waist, washing himself and talking to three foxes chained up to a shed. The foxes seemed to understand his tongue and he theirs, and neither heeded the cart as it drove on. And now, careless of waterfalls thundering among low woods beneath the road, of flames and smoke clouds hunting upwards over the moor, and of mountains such as he had dreamed lying across their course a day ahead, Johnny fell asleep, content, not even rousing himself to make sure whether that was the cuckoo he heard upon the hillside.

The dream of the fixed open eyes wreathed and wavered. Was it the same day — it was morning and about noon — when he stood by the door of a long white inn fronting the sun? The wide courtyard, bounded on one side by the road and on the other by a green hedge, was dotted with fowls pecking idly or lying down. In the midst rose a brown oak, very thick and stiff and well stricken in years, and at its side a very tall gentleman with a fishing-rod was mounting a trap; and the boy watching him and thinking of his wealth and happiness was happier than he. On the hot white pavement by the door all the dogs were lazy in the sun. Each one, except the big, smooth pointer, had a bone, and each snarled as the pointer strolled past. There was a greyhound, a spaniel, a sheep-dog with one eye almost white, a mongrel, resembling both the spaniel and the pointer, and a fox-hound. From time to time the spaniel's puppies — pure spaniels — broke in among the fowls, and the mother raised her head and left the bone under her paws until the pointer re-appeared. It seemed to Johnny that the sun was always full upon that white inn, that the dogs were always lying down there in the sun, and that it had been so and would be so for all time. He longed to have an inn with a white wall facing the sun, and many dogs to take the sun upon the pavement in front. The fisherman drove away.

The father and son walked in a solitary wood upon the side of a steep hill, and at the foot of it was a green vale that wound with the windings of a broad stream running fast, and at the top of the hill, where it was a precipice, hung a castle with trees growing in its crevices, and its windows looked out through ivy thicker than its vast walls down at several miles of the green vale on either hand, at the sun-bathed gloom of the oakwoods of the opposite slope, at the other castles, bleached crags which could be recognised as the work of men only because they were even bolder and more gaunt than the natural crags round about. Sometimes it rained, sometimes the sun shone, and the father and son were glad of both as they gathered blue violets and white sorrel in the dripping and glistening woods. Under the castle wall they sat down, and the father brought out a book and read: "King Arthur was at Caerlleon upon Usk ..." and Johnny began to think of bowmen shooting through the ivy about the windows, of king and queen walking in the grassy courts within the walls, whose roof was the sky. His father told him that the book was written by his countrymen about the heroes of his country, and the child made over to those heroes the glories that had once been Aladdin's, and the Marsh King's, and King Solomon's . . .

The dark eyes gleamed like a thrush's upon her nest when she is watched.

They saw more mountains, and the cart creeping over them and among them, small as a stone upon the road. And by and by they got down by a brook and began to travel upward towards the source. There were clear and dark pools in the brook where the trout darted and the man with them said: "The fish runs away, who knows that man has sinned." They were among steep woods of oak trees as dense almost as grass, all twisted and grey as if made of stone and very old, but based in greenest leaves and flowers of white, of gold, of golden green. The blackbird sang, and the brook gushed, but they did not speak, except that as they left, the strange man said: "This is the Castle of Leaves." Now, there was no longer a path, and the way was over whistling dead grass and grey stones, like ruins of a palace that must have been lofty as the heavens, and when they had gone further still the man said it was "The Castle of the Wind." And now the mist washed over all and hid everything but silvered stones and dead grass blades underfoot, and the rain that was like bent grass blades of crystal, through which for a moment a sheep crept up and crept away again, or a hare, grey as the grass, but blackened as if by fire, leaped up and dived into the wind, the mist, and the rain. Stumbling still among the ruins of the wind's castle, they continued to climb, until the rocks, now tall as a man and so dense that some had to be scaled, came to an end at the shore of a lake which they surrounded — "The Shepherd's Lake." The cry of a raven repeated at intervals from the same spot high up above told them that the mountains rose higher yet and in a precipice. The boy sat upon a rock while the two men went out of sight to the other side; his father to bathe, as he had done twenty years before when a young man. The wind hissed as through closed lips and jagged teeth. The mist wavered over the polished ripples of the lake that resembled a broad and level courtyard of glass among the rough hills. The men were silent, and the sounds of their footsteps were caught up and carried away in the wind. The boy was thoughtless and motionless, with a pleasure that was astonished at itself. He could not have told how long he had been staring at nothing over the lake when, at his feet, his father's head was thrust up laughing out of the water, turned with a swirl, and disappeared again into the mist. He had not ceased to try to disentangle that head from the mist when once more he heard that wailing song that used to make his father so glad, and he himself sang back such words as, without knowing their meaning, he remembered; his brain full of the mists, the mountains, the rivers, the fire in the fern, the castles, the knights, the kings and queens, the mountain boys at cricket, the old man with the foxes, the inn dogs lying in the sun . . . the sun . . . the mist . . . his country . . . not the country he had fought for . . . the country he was going to, up and up and over the mountains, now that he was dying . . . now that he was dead.

The Stile

THREE roads meet in the midst of a little green without a house or the sign of one, and at one edge there is an oak copse with untrimmed hedges. One road goes east, another west, and the other north; southward goes a path known chiefly to lovers, and the stile which transfers them to it from the rushy turf is at a corner of the copse.

The country is low, rich in grass and small streams, mazily sub-divided by crooked hedgerows, with here and there tall oaks in broken lines or, round the farm houses, in musing protective clusters. It is walled in by hills on every side, the higher ones bare, the lower furred with trees, and so nearly level is it that, from any part of it, all these walls of hills, and their attendant clouds can be seen.

I have known the copse well for years. It holds an acre of oaks two or three generations old, the roots of ancient ones, and an undergrowth of hazel and brier which is nearly hidden by the high thorn hedge.

One day I stopped by the stile at the corner to say good-bye to a friend who had walked thus far with me. It was about half an hour after the sunset of a dry, hot day among the many wet ones in that July. We had been talking easily and warmly together, in such a way that there was no knowing whose was any one thought, because we were in electrical contact and each leapt to complete the other's words, just as if some poet had chosen to use the form of an eclogue and had made us the two shepherds who were to utter his mind through our dialogue. When he spoke I had already the same thing in the same words to express. When either of us spoke we were saying what we could not have said to any other man at any other time.

But as we reached the stile our tongues and our steps ceased together, and I was instantly aware of the silence through which our walking and talking had drawn a thin line up to this point. We had been going on without looking at one another in the twilight. Now we were face to face. We wished to go on speaking but could not. My eyes wandered to the rippled outline of the dark heavy hills against the sky, which was now pale and barred with the grey ribs of a delicate sunset. High up I saw Gemma; I even began trying to make out the bent star bow of which it is the centre. I saw the plain, now a vague dark sea of trees and hedges, where lay my homeward path. Again I looked at the face near me, and one of us said:

"The weather looks a little more settled."

The other replied: "I think it does."

I bent my head and tapped the toe of my shoe with my stick, wishing to speak, wishing to go, but aware of a strong unknown power which made speech impossible and yet was not violent enough to detach me altogether and at once from the man standing there. Again my gaze wandered dallying to the hills — to the sky and the increase of stars — the darkness of the next hedge — the rushy green, the pale roads and the faint thicket mist that was starred with glow-worms. The scent of the honeysuckles and all those hedges was in the moist air. Now and then a few unexpected, startled and startling words were spoken, and the silence drank them up as the sea drinks a few tears. But always my roving eyes returned from the sky, the hills, the plain to those other greenish eyes in the dusk, and then with a growing sense of rest and love to the copse waiting there, its indefinite cloud of leaves and branches and, above that, the outline of oak tops against the sky. It was very near. It was still, sombre, silent. It was vague and unfamiliar. I had forgotten that it was a copse and one that I had often seen before. White roses like mouths penetrated the mass of the hedge.

I found myself saying "good-bye." I heard the word "good-bye" spoken. It was a signal not of a parting but of a uniting. In spite of the unwillingness to be silent with my friend a moment before, a deep ease and confidence was mine underneath that unrest. I took one or two steps to the stile and, instead of crossing it I leaned upon the gate at one side. The confidence and ease deepened and darkened as if I also were like that still, sombre cloud that had been a copse, under the pale sky that was light without shedding light. I did not disturb the dark rest and beauty of the earth which had ceased to be ponderous, hard matter and had become itself cloudy or, as it is when the mind thinks of it, spiritual stuff, so that the glow-worms shone through it as stars through clouds. I found myself running, without weariness or heaviness of the limbs through the soaked overhanging grass. I knew that I was more than the something which had been looking out all that day upon the visible earth and thinking and speaking and tasting friendship. Somewhere — close at hand in that rosy thicket or far off beyond the ribs of sunset — I was gathered up with an immortal company, where I and poet and lover and flower and cloud and star were equals, as all the little leaves were equal ruffling before the gusts, or sleeping and carved out of the silentness. And in that company I learned that I am something which no fortune can touch, whether I be soon to die or long years away. Things will happen which will trample and pierce, but I shall go on, something that is here and there like the wind, something unconquerable, something not to be separated from the dark earth and the light sky, a strong citizen of infinity and eternity. The confidence and ease had become a deep joy; I knew that I could not do without the Infinite, nor the Infinite without me.

The End of a Day

TOWARDS evening of that tempestuous day the west began to clear and brighten under a swaying heavy curtain of cloud, and the primroses to shine with a cold light out of the black earth, as I left the road to cross a corner of the moor. Before me and moving athwart my path in the slant rain was a young girl. Though the rain was in her eyes and hair, and the wind enveloped her with its cold kisses, she was young and proud. Her head was lifted up and her lips parted with pleasure at the rain upon them. She had come out at the sight of the brightening west and was walking towards it. She was lightly dressed as knowing, that the rain was spent, or not caring, and she had not gone many steps before me when it ceased. The dark woods behind her still roared with the dying wind and the dripping rain, yet upon the moor there was a walled-in silence through which she walked, and upon her and the dead grass fell a watery cold light out of the white pane that widened every moment more radiantly in the western sky. And to me, losing all memory of the storm and the peace-making, it was as if the day had led up to this, as if a long resounding avenue had led to a still glimmering lawn as broad as the earth and mingling with the bright heavens. I had emerged out of the darkness and mist into an immeasurable and wondrously open world, and across it moved the figure of the girl. My steps became slower and slower. I no longer drove my heels into the ground. My lips ceased to murmur all manner of songs, poems, fragments of tunes, hunting cries, fantastic exclamations remembered or invented. In a minute or two I sat down on a boulder in the grass, and leaned forward wearily with hands and chin upon the handle of my stick.

The girl was beautiful. Breasting the rain at first, and now facing the restful and splendid west, any springy maid might have painted herself upon my brain for an hour or so, But she so raised my thought that suddenly at this noble end of a great day I felt myself weary, at once weary and very glad. Had she leaped out of the earth or out of the sky to express in human shape the loveliness of the hour, she could not have been made otherwise by a sculptor god — solemn and joyous and proud with the pride of things that are perfect and know it not, yet have as it seems attendant spirits offering them praise and courtliness wherever they go. No princess barbarically and multitudinously escorted could have walked with greater magnificence than this girl thinking her thoughtless thoughts. She now was the triumphant one, as I had been when I looked over plain and hill and saw them faint and quiet as in a tale. Not for one moment, but all the time of watching her, I felt as though I were looking out of a grave where I lay stiff and still but with wide eyes and untired spirit, and with those eyes and that spirit saluted and loved the beautiful living creature passing by regardless.

I watched her plant her feet firmly and rise up lightly as one might do to whom these things were impossible and marvellous. She had a slightly swaying motion which, graceful in itself, was fascinating, partly because it suggested how much more so it would have been had she been utterly unencumbered by dress. This swaying from hip to heel was the most obvious expression of the indolence which went side by side with her force, and was one with it, since it showed how much of that force was subdued in the effortless exercise of walking. She could have run, she could have leapt and climbed, almost it seemed that she could have flown, yet she but walked steadily across the moor. She was perfectly at peace, untried by pain and strife and sorrow, or passion.

The unaccomplished hours hovered about her as she went. She might some day be a Helen, a Guinevere, a Persephone, an Electra, an Isoud, an Eurydice, an Antigone, an Nimue, an Alcestis, a Dido, a Lais, a Francesca, a Harriet. She was a violet-eyed maid walking alone. Yet these were the spirits that attended her. Helen whispered to her of Theseus, Menelaus, Paris, Ulysses, of calm Lacedæmon, and burning Troy; Persephone of the lone Sicilian meadows, and the dark chariot and Dis; Dido of Carthage and Æneas and the sweet knife of despair; Eurydice of Orpheus and Hades and the harp and silence; Isoud of Tristram and the ship and joyous Gard; Lais of many lovers, and not one love; Electra of her brother; Alcestis of her spouse and death; Harriet of the poet, and the water that quenched love. And there were many more upon the grass under the western light. They were tempting, guarding, counselling, warning, wailing, rejoicing, vaguely whispering. They waited on her, some wistful, some imperious, but all drawn after her whithersoever she went, all praising her for her sweet lips, her long brown hair and its gloom and hidden smouldering fires, her eyes and her eyelids that were as the violet opened flower and the white closed bud, her breath sweet as the earth's, her height, her whiteness, her swift limbs, and her rippling arms and wrists and hands, made for love and for all fair service; her straightness, that was as the straightness of a tulip on the best day of spring; and for her life, because it was all before her, pale and mysteriously lit, without stars yet with the promise of stars like the sky which had now dismissed all clouds but one dark bar, and was expanding around and above without a bound. Into that sky, into the gorse of the moor and a wild multitude of birds, she slipped out of my sight; and I rose up, and knew that I was tired, and continued my journey.

The Island

FOR several miles two rough brooks from the moorland, gradually approaching one another between rocks that are crowned with forest assume a kind of sobriety and maturity as they widen and feel the sea. The dividing forest descends precipitously in a great wedge to the heron-haunted flats of the confluence. The valley now rapidly grows narrow, and its sides more steep and bare, until vertical rock walls form a gate-way for the river out to the sea. Around the harbour, on the steep sides and floor of the vast chamber between the confluence and this gateway, the town is built. The principal shops, a group of public offices, and an hotel on one side, a few dwellings, a line of warehouses, and a low-towered church on the other, stand in broken rows along the water; and all these are of grey stone with greenish-grey slated roofs. Above and behind these the houses are either perched upon horizontal ledges or appear to be in the act of scrambling up or down to them; they also are of stone, some grey, many white or yellow, and the spaces between them are filled by the green of their precipitous little gardens or the yellow of rock blossoms. Higher still, upon the brink of the valley, are the edges of the pasture and the cornland, and the grey or the stained white walls of one or two farms.

It is low tide. The naked fishing boats or small trading craft lean high out of the clear and unruffled green water, the bronzed weeds, and the white and grey and silver and blue minute pebbles below the quay. Many white gulls float on the water, others are rising or descending, some coil in and out among the masts and above them continually, and are joined by ones and twos and small companies arriving at a great height from inland or low down from the sea. Those that float are silent, those rising or descending or wheeling are crying to one another with sea voices among sharp white pinions.

Near one side of the harbour men in blue jerseys sit or stand in knots, or walk this way and that very slowly among the drying, brown nets and the casks and boxes. On the opposite side a few carts or foot passengers follow the roadway along the edge of the water until it comes to a multitude of oak trunks lying in giant loose bundles. Over these children are always climbing, or hiding amongst them; and, if there be sun, one or two of the oldest men are sitting on the warm timber. To pass the trees the road curves outward a little and then back again to cross a low, long bridge to the little shelterless, empty railway station. Beyond that are the mud flats and the stilted herons, the wedge of oaks, the two valleys and their jackdaws shouting, and, farther still, moorland, moorland, moorland, like a dim, cloud-bank that never moves and is yet never the same. Seaward, this road fringes one of the vertical rock walls of the river gateway, passes round between the sea and a dozen large new houses and private hotels, and where they end becomes a rude track climbing to one grey farm and then another upon the sky-line, where it disappears under a bunch of sycamores.

Opposite the hotels and new houses and their many white-painted window frames between road and sea, is a waste patch covered with bramble and gorse, thistle and tall grass, where a little-voiced bird perches on the top sprigs and twitters with his head turned out to the sea that drowns his song. Up from the waste all day long a meadow pipit rises into the air and slants, singing its wild and delicate song, down past the windows of the hotel. The brambles overhang, a short dip of yellow sand down to a narrow daisied sward and then the beach. There the low western light turns the crumbling grey rocks to gold and brightens the white gulls standing each on a fragment of rock just disappearing under the tide. The water is of an effervescing, infinitely rippled grey blue, but silver at the rock edges where the black weeds heave and unroll.

The sea is idle except on the shore, where it plunges up sighing as if weary of inaction, and in this sigh spends itself as with a broken resolve, so that but a trickle of the wave runs up among, the gorgeous weed-quilted rocks.

The coast is a long curve of grey sand and dark rocks, ending on one hand several miles away in a green headland with a sheer fall like a chin down to the sea; on the other in a grey promontory, so far off that its hazy prostrate line is always upon the utmost boundaries of sight when it is not apparently floating between sky and sea, an invention of fancy, something not of this earth, or such a seaward place as the ancients supposed to be the abode of dead men's spirits. For the most part the sea between these two extremities is divided from the inland by unscaleable scarred red cliffs, to the edge of which the earth is green with corn or grass, except at one point close to the harbour mouth, where it is yellow with charlock like a perpetual sun-stain. Once or twice this wild sea wall is broken for the outlet of a small stream, and there the sand widens, and above is the horizontal white streak of a hamlet. Not more often there is a white spot above the cliffs — a solitary farm. The sea is aflower with little sails, white, old gold, ruddy brown, apparently motionless; but you turn away and look again and they are scattered wide, and two black steamers point towards the promontory; and yet again, the sea is bare, but in the still air the smoke of the vanished steamers hangs in two enormous uplifted wings across a quarter of the sky.

But men, gulls, ships, the enchanted distant promontory, cannot long keep the eyes away from a round island lying almost opposite the harbour mouth, beyond a chain of surf. It is a green hill based upon grey sands. Half of the slopes are grass, the other half is a wood of dark evenly grown pine, whose outer boles take the light like pillars of rosy marble or gold. The blunt summit of the island is clean over the pines. Upon the grass, near the sea and the edge of the wood, is a small white house and a green irregular enclosure with a white wall.

There are times, solitary, cold spring dawns — summer nights of transubstantiating air — twilights of autumn, foreboding but very calm — glistering winter afternoons, when the island, and the white house and wall, the clear pines, the fringe of pale sand and its lace of foam, are but a very little way across the sea, when a lover would wish, and wish so boldly, and with so mighty and fierce a happiness that it seemed possible, to leap, to fly, to travel swiftly as thought over the waves and possess the island for ever with his beloved — to walk to and fro among the trees of noblest poise, whose sound never can cross the sea's whisper or tumult, to lie upon that green grass, to race upon that pale sand, to swim in that sapphire water, to kiss in that bright house — to live, to enjoy, to love, to be forgotten by all the world save only that one beloved for ever. And suddenly the island is gone, somehow swallowed up by rain, mist, snow, or a jealous god.

Though near enough for such a lover's leap the island is not too near the shore. No one ever swims out to it. Now and then a little boat makes towards it for a long time but turns back, because it is not any more near. The windows of the white house are but shapeless dots, which it is hard to number. So one is ever seen upon the pale beach under the low cracked cliff, or in the green enclosure between the white walls. The smoke of the stout chimney ascends blue against the pines like that of another house, and yet with a more divine tranquillity, and as if by magic, for it seems that the house can hardly be inhabited by men. Thus at most hours and to most men the island seems inaccessible. To sail near it is always like being carried by fate past an hour, a place, a person, out of which an altogether strange and perfect happiness might have been gained. The mild grey and white of the cloudland overhead is broken up by blue pits and clefts; the oily, placid sea sways and sways, now blue and now grey, over the reflected azure, in mounded swells without ridges and without foam; discs and patines and rounded long shapes of light upon the water waver amid frames of darker grey and blue, interchanging with them continually; a bird of ebony slips by; between sea and sky there is nothing but your own brooding and dismayed spirit. To land on the grey sand and dismiss the ship . . . but it is never accomplished. The surf bristles upon its girdle of rocks. And presently the island is far away and irrecoverable and grim against the low sun, a barbarous, barren, uninhabited, dark land.

Or a man goes down to the rocks through a soft wind that is all grey rain. A wreath of little birds pipes by and drifts rapidly into nothing. The earth under him is being dissolved into something vague and desolate, into a mist like the sea and sky. A heron detaches itself from the dark rock and pale pool, where it was unseen, and flaps heavily into the enfolding rain without a sound, towards the island, which is invisible before, as the mainland, the beach, the sand wall, the long curve of coast behind are also invisible. He can see nothing but the near rocks, their weedy crevices, the still pools on the shelves, as he climbs and stumbles and zigzags onward and outward, until the gossamer rain seems to begin to shape out of itself a mound — a cone — a shadow — the island — which disappears, as it is completed; and out of this the curlews are crying.

The island is not too near or too far to be the finished idea of an island. In spring it is greener than the most verdurous coombes; among the shadows of the forlorn end of autumn it is the most shadowy. It can be clearly seen, yet it cannot be comprehended. It is beautiful, and it has an air of being inviolate and imperishable. It is sweet and delicate; it is wild also and free. It is far enough to be of another substance than the earth under our feet. A mist sighing out of space unbuilds it: the moon builds it again and delivers it up. It is near enough to be a blissfully exalted and perfected portion of this earth under our feet. It is not out of reach, yet it is never attained. It is not forbidden, and nevertheless something withholds or indefinitely delays it. Some day — somehow — we shall be there and not leave it again; but not yet. It beckons, it waves back, it withdraws itself, it reappears, it expects, it refuses; but evermore it awaits. It is the place for a bridal — or for a grave.

Winter Music

It was the end of the first warm day in February, of the first day when you might lie on a southern slope and do nothing but look into the air as into a well and see the larks looking like minute beetles on the surface of the blue.

The night had been frosty and still, and dawn was yet more still. The sky was of a misty pale blue tending to violet, but fading to an ash-coloured haze low down that hid the hills five miles away on the horizon, though all else was clear. On the eastern and south-eastern blue were thin fragments of distant-looking white clouds, so thin that they might have been painted on the sky from which they hardly stood out at all. Myriads of starlings flew by, straight onward from west to east, midway between earth and sky, and made a black net which entangled the slim wan moon in the south-west like a mermaid caught by fishermen. A kestrel was perched motionless on an ash-tree top, black against the east. The rime was thick on the grass, but thrushes sang clear.

As the sun rose behind the kestrel and the tree, blotting them both out, a little wind was born. Light filled the sky, but with no colour except palest and tenderest gold, and the breasts of the singing birds were golden towards the dawn. The sun itself was a ring, not a disc, of silver, just visible in its own fierce blaze. All the oaks on eastward hillsides showed pale trunks, tier above tier, all the old orchard trees were clothed in gold. In the retired hollows of the near hills the frost was bluish and gave them a far-away look as if they were sky instead of earth.

And now the chaffinches began to sing. Their fresh yet sleepy and invariable tune is appropriate to warm still air, and in this wind over the rime so early in the year they could not deliver their full song, but at first only the three or four opening notes, and then broke off as if they had forgotten and resented it; even when they got past these notes their hesitating song among the apple branches, often repeated in the sun, was like the swallow's trill.

Until nightfall I walked slowly — it was the first day when you could walk slowly since October. The sky was milky blue, with now and then a few passing faint clouds like foam. The woods of beech or oak in the upper parts of the rising land were dry and warm; at their lower edges the ploughlands undulated with grey long waves as smooth as if planed, and seeming almost to roll onward in faint shadow and light. On the turf of the pasture the flints shone as if they were white flowers. The larches in the plantations seemed to have been dipped in pale fire. White gulls wavered over the green corn and rose to fly clear of the isolated beech-surrounded group of farm-buildings and stacks, but alighted on the roof of a little flint church, with a low sharp spire standing out in the middle of a pasture and utterly removed from any other congregation.

The undulations of ploughland and pasture died away in a low, level country of pine and oak forest, paved with the pale leaves of chestnut undergrowth, and pierced by straight yellow roads, and once or twice interrupted by orange gravel pits. Here and there the roof of a solitary house glowed with tiles of olive and ochre and orange amid rough tussocky grass at the edges of the forest. An old grey-bearded man in a greasy, patched, once-white smock was spreading dung, while the larks sang high above and the sparrows scattered low in the dusty gusts around him; then solitude; then another old man alone. In the roadside moss, and among the roots of hazel and thorn, a primrose peeped, half-opened and with no stalk, or a daisy drooped in the shadowed, unmelted rime, the yellow and the white flower very tender like a yet unborn beauty of spring, forerunners lost on their way.

But it was one of those days when what meets the eye is far less than what is apprehended, when a man may spend all the hours of light out of doors and see nothing and hear nothing and yet be profoundly blessed. The birds, the trees, the houses, the few flowers, may indeed be seen, and the songs heard from branch and sky, but all these little things are dwarfed, and, in the memory, sometimes quite shut out by the sense of the presence of earth itself, the huge, quiet, all-sustaining earth mutely communing with the sun. And so it was this day. When at last the sun had set with as little colour and stir as at dawn, and I sat down under a roof, I remembered little, thought of nothing, but I glowed and was at ease, trembling and tingling from the indescribable intimate contacts of the day.

I sat still in a darkening room, whose low long window showed the cliffy wall of the last house of a town, a blurred shrubbery, and, on a rising ground beyond, one cedar whose black storeys of motionless foliage filled half of the pallid sky. The wind had gone away with the sun. All was still, all silent. The sound of the last carriage and foot passenger had passed away from the road running at the foot of the sharp cliff, it seemed, an eternity ago. So silent was it that, though in a town, it was not the mere absence of traffic that awed the brain. All sound had disappeared and was replaced by a beautiful soft silence, omnipresent and omnipotent. This was the perfect state. Never again could it be troubled. All wheels and feet had gone out long ago through the pale gateways of the west, where sun and wind had passed out, and they had gone for ever. The tower was empty. That rigid cliff of wall was dead: it seemed even that it was maintained by the silence, and that if that should be broken it would crumble at the same time to nothing. The great tree against the sky was exalted. I had seen it many times but never thus. It seemed the source of the silence, and out of its caves flowed continually, as a river, the power that was taking a possession of all the earth as the crepuscular light subsided. This was that great silence, the first of things and the last, on which life has intruded for a little while, that great silence which is all about us, and over the edge of it we may step anywhere and at any time, perhaps never to return. Its empire is eternity. Therefore it is very patient, very gentle, very grave, so that the bird or the trumpet knows not the unfathomable ocean into which the sound of its love or its insolence has fallen. As a rule, when we are aware of it, the frontier of it is elusive and moves with us; now it is yonder, across the river, and again it is beyond that lift in the twilight road. But this evening it swept on majestically. The door, a few paces away, opened into the heart of it. The fire burnt low and stirless, because it was on every side. The nearest things, the flowers on the table at my side, the pictures on the wall, were already caught up in it and looked unlike themselves, poor and unboasting, touched as if by death, that most pompous and most venerated of the servants of silence. The tenth wave rose high as the violet heavens and the first star, and were it to plunge all would be overcome. The room was extending indefinitely, and the farther walls fading away under the menacing cave of the wave, when from out of the cedar, as it seemed, a strain of music crept interceding, and the wave did not fall but retired imperceptibly into the tide. The opening notes were slow and musing and delicate, and at any moment they might have ceased, so timorous were they after the silent storm that had lately withdrawn before it. Even so the last few leaves of winter mutter in the preluding breath of spring in which they must die. They were dying away — soon, like the leaves, they would have fallen to rest — and close at hand that great tide was approaching again. The music was almost silent; the notes, the withered leaves, had touched the earth when they began to flutter, to trip, to whirl up; they muttered again, still soft and hesitating, but now not hesitating for fear of death, but because they were not yet sure of their destiny. The sounds were behind a veil like the fragrant coloured flower within the brown bud, or the painted bird in the egg. They paused, moved slowly forward, more softly, coiling now, writhing serpent-like, making for the light which they could not see. These were treble notes more than infantine, innocent, frail, grave, dimly, very dimly, aware of the mighty or terrible things of good and evil to come. Then a deep chord. The light. A glimmer seen underground through the veil, the sheath, the shell, but still a glimmer of light, and the music had seen it far away and was starting, in pursuit, more loudly but gradually. It saw the light, but not what was beyond. It stole away as if in a few moments it would lose itself in what it sought and be gone. But now it was clear, advancing yet more loudly, even with pride, as of arching instep, and hair tossing, but smoothly as over velvet. All went so easily that I thought it would be over and done in a song. The notes, set free, seemed to have forgotten the dreams of a strange destiny. Now, surely, now all is achieved, the music will end swiftly in the flush of childhood, ignorant and careless of itself. But there was a pause, and another grave chord, a cloud summoned above the horizon into the stainless blue. Again there were antenatal whisperings. The crumpled, half-opened primrose by the wayside was not more diffident. The music had gone back into the womb again. That was not the light but the dream of it in the sleep of one who had never seen the light. Again the coiling, the writhing, the little sounds that chipped at the shell in darkness. It was after all to die ere it was born, and the notes wailed, wailed without knowing why, without knowing what they had missed. It asked, Why? and the wail ceased. The music continued, but now it seemed that another creature moved within it — formless, vast, reluctant. The notes were bass and long and slow as of a monstrous bulk stirring in sleep and unwilling to awaken. Soon he slept, and the notes just heaved.

Then it was as if a little bird alighted above the monster, and sang so that he followed the song dreamily in his sleep with a moan of his own dark throat. Still, birdlike, the music swelled as with an innumerable choir, and the sleeper was all but forgotten. Sweet and wild and swift the birds sang melodies that were threshed by the wind, washed by the dew. They sang as if they had never sung before, and as if they were to sing for ever, so eagerly and happily. I knew that multitudinous song, emparadised, remote, serene, only it had never before been so fair, nor had thus changed all the desires and joys of the flesh into this aerial sweetness on keys of ivory and crystal, pipes of reed and gold, strings of gossamer, wreathed horns of exquisite shell, warm throats of beauty, of love, of youth, and of joy. It could not know change. It would build fair towers, soaring high into dawn and into evening, and from their windows would beckon all the lovers of the world, and all the minstrels, glad and at ease in eternity. Yes, it was so. The triumph, the expectation. The music trembled and swayed, delighted and fearless on the perilous edge as when a flower hangs down almost to the earth with dew. Almost, I feared . . . Was it sinking, and to what? Could it rise higher? and if not, must it not fail? Not to triumph yet more was to fail. Surely those towers knew not weariness and could have never enough, nor those lovers don robes of penitence, regret, despair . . . It sank no more. The dew was spilt by a gale and the flower mounted up. The music was awed and hushed, but could not be saddened, for such a time as a bee dwells in one crocus, and then once more the music expanded, leaped up mightily into the speed of the birds' song and the power of the bulk below, of a dragon, enormous, many coloured, glittering. The dragon shouldered himself out of the ground with a great earthquake, and stood for a moment sniffing the air of the mountains, and then bounded up and forward with lightnings on feet as of a stag, and uplifted wings as of eagles. The great plumes winnowed the air with azure and gold and uncounted green, that shone like stars, leaves, and waves, or glowed like flowers. His proud limbs bent under the flanks that were rippled like the sea; his hoofs lit fires in the rocks beneath. His breast of emerald mail took the sun like a broad hill facing the summer south; it yearned forward like a proud ship launched into a sapphire sea and air of crystal. His mouth opened with a dazzle of pearl, and breathing forth a gentle fire he filled the clouds with rose and the earth with music of rivers of content. As his wings towered, the large feathers whistled wild, the lesser tenderly as the linnet or swallow sings; and as they fell they swept the dew softly from leaf and blossom into the grass. He planted his feet upon the crags, upon the tree-tops, upon the shining waters, upon the cross of the sword of Orion in the west. As mild as he was vast, his footprints soiled not a flower. The music, now ever more loud, was gamesome and stately by turns, but even when stately it was half shy of itself, and the purple and gold were all blossomy and the uttermost of the pageant was a rainbow arched from forest to forest over a placid sky. He leapt, he ran, he soared, and always under his feet the illimitable grass and flowers flowing out along his path like a river and many rivulets. His motion was as that of a mountain river mounded and roaring in flood; or sometimes as of a stag running without fear; sometimes as of a birch tree waving. He fed upon the air of the summits and drank their starry springs. Though he went winding like water in a land of hills he went ever forward. The music rose and fell, galloped and thundered; it trotted quietly on rock that gave back a clamour as of many cuckoos to his feet; and it promised never to cease, as how should it do, linked as it was to this mild everlasting dragon?

    Nevertheless his ardour had a little abated since he extruded himself from the rocks. Fed on blue air and liquid crystal, his nature changed. The music was sinking, recalling the earlier hour when the dragon was but listening in sleep to the bird on the branch. Would he sleep in this luxurance of infinite songs and flowers? He ran more slowly and always within the corridors of a wood of green and gold foliage among the ranges of the south. Sometimes he paused or turned aside to gaze at thickets never yet trodden by men. Here the birds' songs were less but the flowers more than ever, nodding above the highest crests of the trees, descending from them in silent cascades to the floor of gold and purple and white upon green. Into one of these thickets he glided and lay down, letting his legs sink under him and his pinions fold under the flowers, until at last the only movement was of his breathing and of the dew which it unloosed from petal and leaf. The radiant and hardy mail, the soaring melodious plume, the limbs of speed, the breast of great power, were buried in a mound of leaves, hidden from the sun save here and there a glance of burnished azure or gold as of a flower. Over him curved the sky, pale as a forget-me-not and without a cloud; the branches of oaks barred it above his head. Behind him the glades through which he had come were deserted save by the flowers he had sown in the prints of his footsteps and the wind that had borne his wings. He slept and no bird of his escort kept watch. Only the woodpecker laughed as he bounded through the air between the glades.

But as before it was a dreaming sleep: only, now, the dreams were not of hope, however uncertain, but of dread. His lair was no palace but a prison, guarded, bolted and barred, by his own fear. Languid but discontented was the music, soft but anxious; and when for a moment it faded it was not because the fear and the discontent rolled away, but because the dragon held his breath to hear. What could he hear? These new notes were but the whisper of the flowers released and rising up after the spilling of the dew — the wings, perhaps, of a few birds who had ventured after the dragon into the solitude of these glades — of the winds released from the wings of their lord. "Hoo-hoo" murmured the wind in the hollow of its hand: or was it a bell perhaps, a bell of marriage or funeral so remote that its meaning could not be known? There was a sighing pause. "Hoo-ohoo-hoo." The notes had something wintry; they had travelled fields of the frost of winters to come, maybe — so wintry that the dragon stirred. An island of azure and gold rose among the flowers: he was awake, though the notes were still so distant and low that they were not yet in this world. But again "ohoo-ohohee-ohohee." This time it must have been from a hunter's horn. It might seem a trick of the north wind's, but the dragon was not deceived. The music crashed as he rose confidently upon his forelegs, raised his wings, and slid forward to a knoll without a tree. He watched with suspended pinions. "Ohoo-ohohee-hoo-oo-oo." It was no longer a moan, but the cruel exultant call of a hunter's horn, not yet hungry and keen, but again and again repeated in careless joy to be mounted and afield under the sun.

Once more the dragon advanced on wings and feet together. He did not fly from an enemy, for he knew none; nor did he go up against an enemy. He felt fear, but it was for the first time, and he knew not that fear may have a cause without. It was something within, awakened by the winding of the horn, that drove him swiftly in wide circles over the land. He was trying his speed and strength and the terror of his roaring plumes, and so great was the speed and the terror and the strength that he ran and soared faster and faster as if he had terrified himself, until at last feeling joyous and confident he stood still at the edge of the precipice that blackened the forest river, in perfect pride, oblivious of his fear and the cause of his awakening.

But the wrathful horn broke in upon the growing silence and serenity. He moved towards it; he circled; he ran, and this time away from the sound, anywhere away from that "ohee-ohohee" sweeping the opulent solitude as with a scythe. Never had his speed and the thunder and terror of it been so great as now; it must have borne down any foe in front no matter how bold. But the foe was behind. The horn ceased. So near were the hunters that the crying of their hounds was heard now in a torrent of joy. The hunters were gathered together. They heard the quarry and their myriad trampling quickly supplanted the dragon's thunder. They foamed into his glades, over the flowers of his lair and along the edge of the river precipice. White and black horses, with solemn eager extended faces, men in scarlet flying mantles, in mail of silver and gold, bearing plumes of many colours and lances set, there was a horse and a man to every tree in the forest. The hounds streamed amongst them like one dappled life, so closely were they packed and so matched their voices. The azure of the dragon beamed for a moment on a hill-top and the music rippled over with ecstasy. Now he and the hunters made one clamour together, as if he were no longer fleeing, but pursuing with them an invisible, inaudible prey.

Sternly they galloped, the white beards, the black and the golden beards and the beardless. He who was first remained first, and he that was next kept the same place, unless he was trampled down, and ever the last rider was the same and he was as swift as the leader. The music that had gloried in the dragon's birth now climbed yet more loftily in the anticipation of his doom.

They rode and he soared and ran as creatures who had found the right way, and followed it with eyes closed to all that lay on this hand or that, bent only on the clattering track and the motion. Oh! joy to hunt, to be hunted, for ever. The chase was all, the end nothing. Regardless of the quarry, they dropped their lances one by one. The music was cruel no more. It was superbly sweet, with a titanic ease. Moor and sea and river and mountain and forest, and again forest and mountain and river and sea and moor. White clouds hunted with them over the blue glades of the majestic sky. Many were the cavernous narrow valleys full of loose stones between the stems of ancient trees long dead, and at their lower end the sea, and at their upper end the forest rising and falling with the mountains which sent down many rivers along those valleys into the sea. Sometimes the chase filled several of these valleys together and was entangled there; or it followed the ridges between them, either seaward to the cliffs, lest the dragon should be among the chasms; or inland and upward to the forest and the mountains and the peaks where the trees could not climb, but whence the hunters, disturbing the sleep, that had looked eternal, of the eagles, could see the dragon deep down and far off in the still ocean of trees below. The river song was drowned by the hooves in the valleys of ever-sliding stones, but the mountain forests were mossy and the crying of the eagles could be heard. The melodies of the hooves were poems and their deep immortal footprints would brim with tales. The music wavered, but only as a cataract wavers that never abates; still vaunting and sonorous it told not of changing hopes, but of ardour always the same, without a doubt or a fear or a regret, without even expectation.

The hunters were spreading out in a longer and longer

chain that was presently no longer a chain, so that the first knew not whether he hunted alone or not, and those behind saw him on his black horse for a moment only when they rose clear on the cliffs above the sea, or at the crest of a mountain descended, or while his horse climbed out of a lake as they plunged in. Of the hounds a few clung to the leader in a wedge; their late companions appeared singly in the ravines howling for a moment ere they disappeared. Not even the leader saw the dragon. Only now and then the sliding of stones in the great distance reached him from the valleys and the laugh of the woodpeckers when the eagles were gone. A wind was rising, and the strength of the music was renewed by storm, by rain and surging forests, and waters round the hidden peaks and the returning eagles, and rivers hunting to the sea. The chase rode on, but no longer knew east from west, nor saw the leader on any summit, nor heard one hound. And some rode east, some west, some north, some south, and all madly, silently, when the clouds began to be seen through the rain, and the blue between the clouds, and in the blue the first stars. Now the horn sounded again and was answered. One by one over many ridges and up from the sea, and from many ravines, those that could hear and ride were returning.

They were in the forest of the dragon's lair again and there were now two chases, for the echoes began among the mountains; and both were phantoms. The forest or night or the echo was troubling the hunters. They scattered, they paused and turned every way. A horn was blown, and another. They were calling one another yet seemed to remain separate like stars. No one saw anything now but the sky overhead and the nearest tree, and the calling grew fainter and the intervals longer. One by one they feared lest they should meet the dragon. The horn ceased, afraid of the long echoes sinking and sinking into the leagues of hills. There was no noise of hoof or cry of horseman. A branch cracked and a silence followed as the rider stood still, afraid. They hunted no more. They lit separate fires among the trees and the crimson flame slit the black night, then fell, and the glow was like the hollow of a huge mouth in the gloom. The bold hunters were lying down to sleep beside their fires; the less bold leaned on their elbows or stood with backs to the fire; and sleeping or awake, they watched continually. At times the glow or a flicker lighted up a leaf, or a brilliant bird, or a wave of the river; and, awake or asleep, the watcher started. But he did not start, nor stir, nor breathe, nor shut nor open an eyelid, when the light showed not a leaf or a bird, but the mail of the dragon as he glided amongst them, and down to the river to drink under the precipice. Past the fires of the hunters he descended, careless of the sleepers and the dreamers who watched. Once more he peered into the thicket where he had slept, but his flowers were gone and the leaves lay on the earth instead of moving against the sky. He mounted the knoll once more and looked round. He listened. The hoot of an owl wandered like a dream of the hunters among the mountains to the moon. The dragon slowly unfurled his wings and launched himself above the waves of the tree-tops and rising in tranquil circles vanished beyond the moon.

And as the music died away and the silence yet did not return, I saw that the lamps were lit, that the curtains were drawn to shut out the cedar tree, the stars, the silence and the gentle words of the owl that were as bubbles out of the silence.

July

THERE were certain periods in Lawrence Garlon's past life, some of them but a few days, others several months long, which had become in his memory foreign countries, each with a sky, an air, and physical character of its own; and as he had much leisure he returned to these countries — the country of January to October 1875 for example, the country of May 1888 — every year several times. Year after year they changed and rose or fell slightly in his favour. Sometimes, as he well knew, the changes were made in imperceptible ways by himself. But a few he could have sworn were the work of other powers than his own.

The most changeful and alluring of all these lands was the nearest, the country of January to October, 1885, to which he was admitted by a score of diverse gateways, and the gateway he most used was that of July. The partner of his journey was always the same, a girl of his own age. And the day was her twentieth birthday, his own being then not many days past. He was so much fascinated by this land that he would at times do the forbidden thing — knock, and having no answer, force open the gate into it; but that meant misery, and he could see the desired only in fragments like trees and haystacks above level mist, and she showed him only glimpses of her smiles, her tears, her white dress fluttering among endless trees that engulfed her as night does the solitary wandering bird. But if there was one time when the bolts were more likely than at any other to be self-drawn and to disclose the vision, it was the first day in January when change from frost and north-east wind and cold rain to warmth, blue sky, white clouds of gracious form and golden light among naked trees, relaxes the sinews, and, while inviting men to some unusual effort, refuses the energy. It was on such a day that he had the journey which completely changed him, by making of him no longer a melancholy but a sad man; nor did he ever think afterwards of knocking impatiently at the gate of July.

The afternoon had been silent, but now, though several thrushes were singing, the silence had become a strong and austere spirit which nothing could disturb. A traction engine struggled up the road that threaded the beech-wood upon the hills, but its sound was outside the sphere of the silence. He looked from hill to hill, to the twenty-mile distant headland carving the farthest silver in the south-east, from cloud to cloud, and from star to star. He followed the flight of a crow until it seemed to descend into the ashes of the west. He listened to the voices of some children in the wood and clung to them almost fearfully as they went farther and farther away fading deep into that other world beyond the enveloping silence. And he sighed as he walked slowly in this quiet, unearthly world. He sighed, too, as he sat down by his own fire, and the gateway of the July country was opened to him. The gateway was opened, but he could not, as he had always been used to do, pass over the threshold. He could only look in and see wandering there another self, the self of July in that lost year, and that wraith was enjoying Margaret as he had done once upon a time.

At the side of this wraith he saw Margaret, whose world this also was, and, for all he knew, her only world, for she was dead long ago. And was not that one of the dead walking with her? He was equally distant and out of reach and recall, and in the sunlight of that land his eyes could not distinguish the ghost of the living from the ghost of the dead. She was tall and carried herself with gentleness and at the same time an animal freedom of movement and gesture; her strength and energy had so far found no way to express itself, except in exquisite grace, buoyant head, bright eyes, and a habit of interrupting her walk by running or tripping unconsciously for a few steps; and few could have looked at her without thinking what noble children she might bear, or without a sigh that she could not be thus everlastingly. He at her side was taller, fair-haired and more frail, and it was only his passion that for the moment made him worthy to be with her; already the weakness might have been detected that made him fitter to lament her loss in a study than to reign as her lover.

As she used to do, years before, she flowed beside him swiftly, and with a motion as if she trod not upon the earth, but upon the south wind that was always blowing in that land. Her brows and the dark brown hair crowning them were on a level with his eyes and often did he look at them.

At first there was a long ascending road, broad and dry, but with a dryness that could be enjoyed, as one of the truest pledges of summer, from the shade of the hawthorns alongside. The dew was still on their leaves, and on the grass of untenanted gardens seen betwixt the stems. The two looked together at these solitudes and smiled, knowing that there were others more deep, more cool, and fuller of sunlight, beyond. Sometimes the two looked in one another's eyes and hardly waited to kiss, he laying his two hands on her two cheeks, and she pressing his hands so tightly with hers that her lips pouted under the kisses, and she would slip one of his arms about her neck, and keep it there while they walked, their heads erect, in the green gloom of old trees that were the mansions of other lovers, invisible, melodious, but heeding them not. Or she looked at him, but he at the trees ahead, trying hard not to notice her for a little time, but knowing well that a smile was already forming on her lips, and delaying for its perfect flourishing till he should turn and behold, which, not too late, he did, and turned two smiles into one kiss. More seldom it was that both looked ahead, and that he was the first to turn, and every time she also turned and caught his eyes just as they were settling on cheeks or shoulders with butterfly glances. He could not have said why they walked on and on, why their lips ever deserted one another, or their arms disentwined themselves, or their eyes shook off one another's magnetism, why they did not stop and demand an eternity of embraces. Yet rarely did they pause in their walk for more than a moment, for longer than a bird's song or than a bee's visit to one flower.

But Laurence knew — the watcher, and not the lover — and he stared nevertheless more and more eagerly as if to know what they would do.

When they wished to feed their eyes or lips more boldly, she stooped for some purple or golden flowers out of the grass and asked him to fasten them at her throat, or, those being withered, she stood on tiptoe and plucked a rose and carried it, or he cut a long strand of bryony and wound it as a crown in her hair. While they were passing one of the gardens she stayed behind — actually he went on two steps without her — and she unfastened her hat, sending both hands bird-like to the back of her head on the errand, thus tempting him to pounce upon her lips while they were without the pretence of protection. She took off her hat and covered it up with nettles until they should return, and so all day long he had to wind fresh crowns of bryony and wild hops to shield her head, or when they sat he covered it with a huge burdock leaf, bespangled with spray from the rivulet — just as the watcher had done twenty years before. These were the same roses, roses twenty years old, so cool to the finger-tips, yet glowing and misty warm with love and summer, their golden or dark hearts moist with dew, pure and fresh and sweet, yet not more pure or fresher or sweeter than her fingers that gathered them, or her throat against which they pressed their petals as she strained for the topmost. Over their heads was bent an immortal sky. Not all the years could stain the blue of that sky. Lofty, and based upon infinitely far-off hills, it was nevertheless their sky: it was good and kind to them, and blessed their love and their spring lust: out of it had descended so many resplendent days that those before were forgotten and those yet to come were inexhaustible: like the floor of this their palace of the earth it seemed to have been built to receive them, and they saw it with a sense of possession, and, measureless though it was, it was less so than their love, their joy, their hope, their immortal life.

The fire cracked and crumbled at the watcher's side with a noise prophesying frost; he shivered as he looked into the summer land where the south wind blew. And now they were alone upon a wide moor.

Margaret walked among the purple heather and the yellow gorse. The blue sky praised her white form, her green-coroneted brows. The black flashes of her eyes lightened at her lover's out of the pale rose of her cheeks. When she was looking he could not keep his eyes away from hers, and they fenced together as if the aim of love was to prolong that airy bickering. When she was not looking, for a moment only, his eyes wandered to the divinely warm and tender skin like a flower under her ear and her looped hair, but not often dared to kiss it because it was too sweet. He was as happy, though the thought never came into his head, when he was gazing away, straight ahead, not even holding her hand, as when it seemed impossible for them ever to end their embrace or love's silent duel of eyes.

Why, thought the watcher, why does he ever look away? Why will he not consume her with kisses and not wait so timorously? It is not many days before she is to die. Why will he let her go on staring piercingly in front of her, as though her eyes saw through the blue and through the forest now gathered about and before them in groups and masses and solitary trees? For, look, the smile almost dies from her lips and cheeks; if she looks a moment longer she will perhaps discover the spectre with that burning glance. Ah, he has kissed her; she has detached her eyes from the horizon as if she had not seen anything all the time but his face, and smiles as if she had been wilfully looking away.

At the edge of the forest, where the golden light was melting but never surrendering to the golden gloom, the lover knelt down, keeping one of her hands in both of his and covering his face with it, while she laid her other fingers upon his head and watched him with trembling lips and eyes in which the fires looked as if they could not shine brightly and tenderly enough without some tears. Fiercely he pressed her hand upon his eyes to shut out all sight and thought — now, even now, why will they not make an end or the earth swallow them up? — but, presently, stung perhaps by the fragrance of her flower-gathering hand, he rose again, and, not turning to her, as if some thought had come to him that was not for her — and yet that was impossible — he led her on by the finger-tips to the deeps of the forest, a forest as old as the earth itself, and wearing its age heavily and with groans and a lowering aspect. But those two descended into it without fear, joyfully and exultantly. Its only limit was the sea, which they never saw but heard all day long making a sound like the murmur with which silence fills too wakeful ears. To those lovers the sound was only part of their realm of light and fragrance and melody. Perhaps he would say, "It is the sea," and she reply, "Yes." But neither said, or even thought, "Let us go to the sea." For the sea was beyond, away from them, and it was where they were that love dwelt with joy, and they were not in search of anything that they knew, and therefore the sea was as a poet's tale.

To the watcher it was not the sea, at least not any earthly sea of sunlit sapphire and foam. To him it was the sound of the flight of time, which, never ceasing but heard oftenest at night or in solitude, is for ever lying in wait to spoil men's singing when those songs are not made so that the refrain may be droned by time. If it was a sea, it was that "unfathomable sea whose waves are years" of which the poet speaks. Could those two not tell the difference between the undying moan of those waves and the sound of ocean? He at least knew that if a man listened curiously he could disentangle out of seeming senseless murmur the lamentation of his own death bell. M-m-m-m—sh—ah! They heard it not, or only once she said, "That is the waves, yet there is no wind."

If they did not hear the moan of the unearthly sea, it was as certain that they did see him who was peering upon them out of the twilight gate, out of a desolate heart, nor hear the footsteps which tracked theirs as they floated on or as they paused to kiss. He strove within himself to tell them, to warn, to bid them haste; to let them know — something; but he was not sure what to do, for sometimes he saw that their joy was unshadowed, and for a moment dreaded lest they should detect him; but more often he wished them to know their happiness, to make more of it, not to linger so upon the way as if it would never end any more than they would ever weary.

He sings! He is singing of the most pitiful sorrow—

O bonnie, bonnie was her mouth,
And cherry were her cheeks,
And clear, clear was her yellow hair,
Whereon the red blood dreeps.

Then wi' his spear he turn'd her owre;
O gin her face was wan!
He said, "Ye are the first that e'er
I wished alive again."

It was the ballad of Edom o'Gordon that tells of a castle long ago surrounded by enemies, when the lady of it and her children, but not the lord, were within; and the enemies set fire to it and waited; and the smoke was smothering the mother and children on the battlements, and she let her fair daughter down, rolled in a sheet — let her down on to the enemy's spear — so that he turned away from his victim, and said—

>I cannot look on that bonnie face
>As it lies in the grass.

In their fond happiness the two lovers dwelt long upon these verses, and he must needs repeat them that he might see her turn to hide her tears and kiss them away.

"Do you cry because the verses are sad?" he asked.

"Oh, no, but because they are beautiful," she replied.

They were now deep in the forest, and the third saw them go many paces silent as the trees, sunk into the great silence, a happy part of it, and then emerging from it and glad to see one another again as if newly met. The youth's hands were warm from the sun, but one was warmer where it lay over her shoulder or curved under her further arm to her bosom; and almost it appeared once or twice that she could not support that bliss, for she put his hand away and let her head sink back upon his breast so that he kissed her throat where it was hot from hiding in her dress and from the turbulence of her heart, and his lips dwelt upon the strands of flesh that heaved under them with sighs.

The footpath was over level ground, upon mossy turf or dead leaves, and so narrow that one of them was always brushing a foot through the dark foliage of dog's mercury that enclosed the path as in straight banks where the beeches forbade anything else to grow: it wound in and out, clear cut like the flat bed of a streamlet, the earth pressed firm but not sunken. A little way ahead and behind it was invisible, so that it seemed to open for their passing and then to close over it again. And yet myriads had trodden it: the leaves were not more numerous than the vanished footsteps or their words. Nor was the watcher the only ghost hovering in that amorous and mortal air, though it was he alone that beheld the others. One less intimate with that wood might have thought the hovering forms born from the suggestion of knot-holes or scars on the tree trunks, curious arrangements of branches and of dancing insects or shadows. To him they were a thicket of the phantoms of living and dead upon whom these lovers trod, through whom they wafted their gossamer way, who looked down at them from trees and up from grass and fern and whirled like vapours feebly and without purpose. But Laurence and Margaret saw these faces no more than they heard the sea or saw the spectator of all sitting with blood yet warm and watching beside the dying clicks and sighs of the fire. He shivered as he saw the two come now through bunches of meadow-sweet and wild mint that had to be crushed underfoot, down to a wide pool, half in shade and half burnished by the sun, surrounded by tall reeds and reflecting the reeds, the branches of the forest, the clouds, and their two faces but not those of their companions.

The two bent to drink. They bathed their hands. They sat upon a boulder and dipped their feet into the water and laughed together for the first time, as the cool touch of the element set them free from the net of all but too much love which their kisses had woven.

They were now perfectly still in the midst of those dim whirling multitudes and perfectly silent, girdled in that dense summer murmur, inaudible to the full brain or fancy, through which crept the deeper noise of the sea. The forest came right up to them and stretched its roots out into the water at their feet; but on either side and in front of them the mossy-footed beeches had drawn back a little way from the mirror — leaving however, their images — down to which there was a slope of turf; between these enormous trees could be seen the long green corridors to be travelled at evening. Those two sat confident, as if enthroned, in the heart of this majesty. Here, for their observer, culminated the exuberance of beautiful human and natural life, in this repose. Beyond, perhaps many steps beyond, was the precipice, or slow descent; for it is the careless prodigality of happy life that makes possible death and the tragedy of death; it can ascend no farther, yet it cannot pause; a touch, therefore, and the precipice is under the leaping foot. Life paused for its rhyme to meet it — death. The maiden laughed.

The watcher fixed his eyes upon her in suspense that he might watch every step. But the smile was still upon her eyes and lips when she and her lover and the pool and all the July land ceased to be visible, and had given place to a low, grey winter sky and a flat white winter land, and in the midst of it, under a yew tree, a man, shoulder deep in the ground, casting up dark earth on to the snow at a grave's edge. Of the other land nothing remained save the moaning girdle of that invisible sea; the ghosts had gone. The man paused from his work to say, " 'Tis a beautiful day for a funeral; 'Tis a maid, and she has a white day for her burying...."

"Imbecile!" the watcher tried to say while rushing forward to bury the grave-digger in his own pit, but his hand struck against the cold arm of his chair, he opened his eyes and saw only black branches stirring in the pale south where the moon quivered, now white and very small and half way through her climb.

Hawthornden

HAWTHORNDEN was always home to tea, except once, and it was a significant exception.

When he was about thirty-five Hawthornden moved out into the country, partly because rents were less and he could have a governess for his three children, and so put off for some years the difficulty of choosing a school; and partly, but this was unconsciously, because he had few friends left. As a young man, clever above the common, reckless (within certain limits) and open-handed, he had attracted men of very different types, both at the university and in his bachelor lodgings. But after he married at twenty-eight, his friends never came to see him, except when they were definitely asked to dinner, though his wife was charming and clever and anxious to meet them, and though he was not too fond of her to attend to them. He seemed to have stiffened and chilled. His smile began to have an awkward catch in it. It was so awkward that it ought to have been dignified, but was not quite. And at the same time as his friends were neglecting him he was not making any progress in domesticity. He had decided against entering a profession, and as he could live on his private means, he was at home very much. But there he gave himself up chiefly to solitary reading, and saw his wife chiefly at meals, and, on evenings when he wished to go early to bed, after dinner. He had thought of writing, but he was squeamish and touchy, and had destroyed his early verses and prose with great care, burning them in his room one summer evening, with a tense, red face, and then, by an after-thought, preserving the ashes in a small cherrywood box. He read many books of almost every kind, except criticism. Criticism he had taught himself to hate, because it seemed to him absurd that the writing class should not only produce books, but circulate its opinion of them among people occupied — like himself — with the business of living at first hand, not at second hand. In the days before criticism life and literature had both been finer things. It was the men with no standards of taste at all who made the arts of the great periods. When there was no one to tell men what to put on their walls, how to build their houses, what to wear and what to read, the glorious things were being created which men instructed at every turn in these matters were content to imitate. Hawthornden sought to recover this freedom by allowing no middleman between art and himself as a human being. As it was, however, physically impossible to keep pace with modern literature without a guide, he neglected it without noticing that this was a concession; and as the old literature had been well sifted by the efforts of the very criticism he despised, he had little left but to enjoy, and he discovered, with some annoyance, that he read and thought — so far as he could express himself — very much like everybody else. Nevertheless, he continued to read abundantly, and for the sake of books put off year by year the problems which his own life offered him. He got out of touch with his wife, ignored her friends and only by an insincere though, determined effort, from time to time, succeeded in quieting her hysteria and relieving her melancholy. As to his children, he made spasmodic and more and more conscious efforts at pleasing and understanding them, and, observing that they could do without him, he plumed himself upon their ingratitude, and left them to the natural methods of his wife, of which he expressed his disapproval from time to time. Yet he was fond of the poetry of passion. He would look up from a poem sometimes and see his wife reading or embroidering, and then take his eyes away with a sigh and only the faintest dissatisfied recognition that he was becoming more and more incapable of being passionate himself and of meeting the passion of another. He also continued to sigh for the simple antique attitudes of the emotions in their liberty, and cursed a time when they could only be seen travestied on the stage. It was literature, nevertheless, and the stage, that had given him the standard which he unconsciously applied to scenes in life which he thought should have been heroical, for example, and were not. Nor was he shaken from his dim-pinnacled citadel of unreality by his one experience of something near tragedy at home. His wife rushed at him one day, with stiff, drawn, red-spotted face and staring eyes, and a shrill voice he had never heard before, to tell him that one of the children was injured. He drew her head to his breast and kissed her hair, and felt at first a kind of shame, then an instinctive disgust at the stains and rude prints of her grief. The same with beauty. He could not have defined it, but he had a standard which he applied to loveliness like a yard-wand, and never suspected that it was the standard that was wanting. It was expression that he feared in living beauty. He wanted the calm of antiquity — of death — of the photographs of celebrated women. A dark face, burning and wrenched with eagerness or delight, disturbed him, and — was not beautiful, because he had been at the trouble of putting aside the expression, and observing that the nose was too small, the eyes unequal, the lips too full, and so on.

He was fond of reading fairy tales and books for and about children, and had acquired strong opinions as to what they needed and liked. He was a great lover of liberty, of liberalism, of freedom for thought and action. He could be heard late at night reading aloud in a deep voice poems on liberty, and even at breakfast would relieve himself by muttering impressively —

> And in thy smile and by thy side
> Saintly Camillus lived and stern Atilius died.

The children looked up and said, "What did you say, father?" or "Do say some more like that"; but he stirred his tea, and made haste to leave the table for the study. He admired books of curious character and adventure, such as Borrow's and adored the strange persons who frequented once upon a time, and perhaps even now, the inns and roads of England. He was indignant with civilisation which threatened to extinguish such men, and used to cut from newspapers passages describing the efforts to chain up gypsies and tramps.

When he moved into the country he was prepared for adventures. Gypsies should be allowed to camp near his house and he would be familiar with them. He would invite the tramps into his study for a talk and a smoke. He used to sit by the roadside, or in the taproom of an inn, waiting for what would turn up. But something always stood in the way — himself. He grew tired of paying for a tramp's quart, and was disconcerted, now by too great familiarity and now by too great respect. When a tramp came to the back door, his maids or his wife reported it to him, and they sometimes had interesting fragments of a story to relate;

for the women had human sympathies along with unquestioning commonplace views of social distinctions. Sometimes he saw the man coming or going, and formed romantic conjectures which made him impatient of what he actually heard. He thought at one time that perhaps his mistake was in keeping too near home; he would walk far over the hills, and stay away for a night or two. But it was always the same. He dressed negligently and carried a crooked stick, and when he complained of his failure to get at the heart of the wayfaring man, his wife flattered him by saying that any one could see, what he really was, whatever his disguise; he liked the flattery, and remained discontented.

Perhaps his whole plan was wrong. He had bought many maps, special walking clothes and boots, compact outfits, several kinds of knapsacks, rucsacs, haversacks, satchels, uncounted walking sticks, just as in other departments of his life he found himself buying pipes suitable for this purpose or that, half a dozen different species of lamps, pens, razors, hats and so on. He tried simplicity for a while, but this also meant a new outlay, and he was soon unfaithful.

Among the people of the neighbourhood he received a reputation for unconventionality. He was said to know the country and the people better than anyone. He was mistaken for a genius, a poet, an artist, a Bohemian, an eccentric millionaire, especially as he had a genuine dislike to parties and picnics and to the sound of men and women trying to put emotion into the words, "Isn't the weather perfectly glorious?" by drawling them or emphasising one word or each word in turn. He liked the mistake.

But one thing, above all others, gradually disturbed him. He was always home to tea.

He liked a certain kind of tea — the milk or cream of a precise quantity poured out first into his cup and then the tea on top of it, to scald it and produce a colour and flavour otherwise impossible. Then the sweet home-made cakes . . . Once or twice he went into cottages for tea, to chat with the poor and see them *au naturel*. But he saw nothing, and was therefore keenly alive to the fact that the tea was bad, and the cakes all but uneatable — so that he had a second tea when he arrived home. Mrs Hawthornden was glad of this; she liked him to enjoy himself, and to praise her cakes. She made cakes regularly, and saw that they were of the kinds he preferred. When he started early for a long walk, she used to ask him when he would be back. "Oh, I cannot possibly say!" he retorted at once; but added, on reconsideration, "But perhaps by four or five." He was rarely later than four, and she smiled. He made special efforts not to be back by five — dreading the habit — and yet at last walked so hard as to tire himself in the effort to reach home at that time. So at last, when his wife asked the question, "When shall I expect you back?" he used to say, sometimes smilingly, sometimes with a submissive despair, sometimes with irritation, "Oh, I am always home to tea!" When he was not punctual, he was proud — but regretted the cakes — and read Borrow with greater relish. But the next day he would find himself home again to tea, and eating too many cakes with equanimity. He knew they were too many, and the thought at length prevented him from enjoying them, but not quite from eating them; there was a relic of virtue in this inability to enjoy them, though he knew that it might have been greater. At times, in an ancient cathedral or in the midst of a tragic tale, he started with the thought that he was almost forgetting his tea, and then his pleasure was at an end. Lying awake at night, he reproached himself, "You are always home to tea." He was haunted by it, as men of noble families of old time were haunted by their fate, and in his moments of complacency it crept suddenly upon him.

One day he went out to a distant part of the county to explore a ruin. It was a fine August day, and he spent most of it in the castle. He left it late in the afternoon, and then began to run. There were several trains that he might have caught; nevertheless, he ran. That day he did not return to tea. His wife looked out a train, and expected him first by one and then by another. It grew dark, and he was not back. The afternoon had been hot, and he had run too fast for a man of his build. He was found lying beside the path. He had achieved his ambition. He had not only not come home to tea, but had ceased to think about tea, so far as can be known. He was dead.

The Artist

THIS, said Adams to himself, staring strangely at the dry brushes and blank paper before him, this was the fairest day of the whole year, the youngest child of a long family of days, each fairer than its elder. First, there were two days following suddenly, hot and cloudless, upon weeks of storm, of sullenness, and of restless wind and rain vexing the new leaves and scattering the blossoms; and at the end of the second a thunderstorm out of the east ascended lightly and travelled rapidly away without silencing the birds, though the trees were but as reeds in the current of the wildly streaming, visible wind. The night was cloudless, but with few stars. The day after emerged hazy and moaning, but grew slowly into a prime of breadth and splendour without blemish, and sank into a night of steady raining. The next day, and another and a third, were the same, saving that they developed with different rapidity and by unequal stages of mist, breeze, and again mist, before their triumphs of burning brilliance in the sky and joyful multitudinous profusion crowding upon the earth. The nights were misty and troubled over the days which they entombed and cradled. Adams found himself waiting day after day for the end and crown of this energy and change.

There came a lustrous morning early assailed from all quarters of the sky in turn, as if the heavens were besieging the earth, by thunder and after long, brooding intervals, thunder again and again, now with cannonading and now one boom or blast followed by no sound except its echo and the challenge of the pheasants. The lark in the sky, the blackbird in the isolated meadow elms, the nightingale in the hazel and bluebell thickets, sang on; and before the last of the assault Adams set out, inwardly confident in the day's future.

He walked steadily, but more and more slowly, into the broadening and deepening beauty of the great day. So hot was it that the heat alone would have made him happy, and yet the east wind urged him to go on and on. He forgot that it had ever been cold; it no longer seemed possible that it should ever be cold again; and he was at ease in flesh and spirit, as a creature born for the earth. Now and then he looked at the complicated pale green overflowing the wooded coombes, or at the clouds, stars, or clots of white flowers along the hedges, or at the barley nodding all ways upon already a yard of grey green translucent stalks in the fields above the hollow lanes; and he looked with the calm, experienced, and (he hoped) not jaded eye of an artist turning forty. But, as a rule, if his eye fed it was in pure and independent wantonness, reporting nothing to the brain but pleasure. His eyes did as as they listed, wandering or nesting on this hand and that. Adams, in fact, was a heavy and solid body moving through this luxuriant woodland country of deep lanes, gentle hills and short views, for the benefit of those imps and elves, his two eyes. They delighted, as if they had been but ephemeral creatures and not instruments of an immortal soul, in the silkiness and darkness of the long grass, in the towering of one tree, the forking of another, and the inexplicable ramifications of hundreds; in the flight of the swift which was as if the arrow and bow had flown away together. Rarely were his ears allowed a little play, to collect the round notes of the cuckoo, the raptures of the nightingales, the calm, easy fluting of the blackbirds.

But satiated with the earth of morning, noon, and afternoon, his eyes tended more and more to the sky. There in the north, were clouds, farther away than he had ever before seen clouds, the most delicate of toppling marble mountains, grey-white with a glistening white profile towards the sun, and midway between him and these were a few long, thin strands of a dark blue-grey lying horizontally. Round about the sun itself hung a mass of this blue-grey, edged with fiery gold; and at times that mass disappeared, leaving the sun — as if all that cloud were the fuel of its fury — a dazzling white conflagration filling a quarter of the sky. He walked as if he were going to walk into the heavens beyond the hills.

Again, his eyes fell to the earth. For the first time in the day they dwelt on human faces. It was in a short village street ending at a churchyard, a street of uniform old brick cottages with flat fronts right upon the roadway — all but one, and that had a tiny bow window which seemed all glass. In this window a white-haired woman stood talking to a dark girl, looking straight at her with eyes and lips together, while the girl's eyes, somewhat abased, looked out on to the street. Adams saw chiefly her white dress and her dark eyes, because they were fixed on him and even followed him, yet without the least curiosity or understanding. "Little and brown and lovely is my love," were the words of his thought as he passed by, but he did not know whether they were remembered or inspired. It was a good group, quite apart from the fact that the girl was beautiful.

Past the church, only just out of the sound of the sermon, Adams sat on a gate. The wind had gone away, perhaps up into the sky to comb out the white clouds into curled fleeces; the air below was still as thought. Lowering his head, he saw nothing nor thought of anything, so far as he knew, for an unmeasured space of time. Suddenly a noise of many cattle running in the field behind drew his eyes that way. They had disturbed whatever was going on in his head, and he got down and was almost past the gateway when he glanced once more into the field, and saw white on the other side of it — a girl in white — certainly the girl who had stood in the bay window. A youth in black was leaning beside her over a gate, and stroking some cart-horses. She very soon grew impatient, and for a time stood with her back to them, though they snuffed her hair. But seeing that her companion took no notice, she raised the arm nearer to him and caught his, and tried, without any physical effort, to draw him away from the gate, that they might walk on. At that moment she seemed to Adams to be a little older than her lover, twenty perhaps, while he could not have been more than eighteen. He did not move. Then she took one step away still holding his arm, and with her eyes upon his face, but in vain. So she slid her hand down to his, and made another step away, and a second, still looking up at him; and thus their two arms were now fully stretched out. At the end of the field, several windows, under white-edged gables, looked at them out of the vicarage, from which they had probably come. The youth felt their gaze; for her, the house might have been swallowed in the earth, the earth itself might have been swallowed up, without troubling her eyes or her heart. Only when she bent her head and kissed his imprisoned hand did he face her and give way, and begin slowly to walk alongside of her from the gate. The horses thrust their heads far out, and he turned round; he would have gone back, had she not taken his hand in both of hers, bending as she did so and fastening her eyes upon his, and, as she thought, upon his soul; whereupon he threw up his arms suddenly, and sent the animals racing away.

All her movements were beautiful. By the side of the stiff youth in black she was like a wave lapping at a rock. Adams stood quite still, watching her through the sprays of hawthorn at the edge of his gateway. He had grown happy and breathless in her beauty, and yet sad to see her actions as of one who had given all to one who had not and could not. It was her lover's dog that had set the cattle running, and when it did so again his shout of command was clear, hard, and controlled. She, Adams knew, could not have shouted so. She was strong, spirited, and without fear, but she was too gentle, he thought. Her yielding gestures were still imperious, and the two were now walking slowly and close-linked — she smiling as she took strides equal to his — but in a few days, in a year . . . Yet Adams drew some lines upon paper to remind him of her body bent and head raised when she clasped her lover's hand in both of hers. He watched them receding, and did not take his eyes off them until they had rounded a corner and passed wholly out of sight.

Starting at length to continue his walk, he looked at the sketch abstractedly. He was not a great or even a much-praised artist; he was not a vain man; yet suddenly came into his mind an entirely unforeseen and unfamiliar thought — "Perhaps these pencil marks will endure until after those two lovers are old and after I am dust." He sighed involuntarily, and immediately smiled self-consciously at the absurdity and apparent vanity of the thought. Then, while his mind was occupied he knew not where, with a grave look he tore the paper into many pieces, and dropped them into the ditch, so that they should not disfigure the grass.

Barque d'Amour

A GREAT street organ, adorned with a coloured print of the battle of Waterloo across its upper half, stood opposite a butcher's shop. The organist, dragger and player in one, was with it in the gutter. He did not look in the least musical: his face was small, oblong, and bony, and thickly sprinkled with the gritty beginnings of whiskers, moustache, and beard, of the colour of brick-dust; his eyes were blue and watery; his teeth pressed together to silence their chattering in the cold rain; his thin lips curled into a leer of mixed hate and timidity, in the shadow of a perfectly new check cap like a jockey's. With his left hand he turned the handle of the instrument; his right was deep in the pocket of a blue overcoat which had once belonged to a broad and protuberant gentleman. His eyes roved from window to window in the street, and from back to back of the passers by, returning not to the organ, but to the whole sheep, the joints, and the boxes full of fragments, in the butcher's window. Nevertheless, as he turned the handle the organ emitted the same sounds as if a musician or the original owner of the overcoat had been playing it.

Many people were passing up and down the street, which was narrow, paved with noisy stones, and lined with small shops of many kinds. It ran diagonally from one important street to another, so that the passengers were half of them poor women and children shopping, and half of them men of all classes taking the short cut and walking rapidly, without looking to right or left.

Children stopped and stared at the battle of Waterloo and the grandly dressed but bleeding cavalry, turning now and then to the performer, to envy him the organ and yet observe that he was not proud of it, and that he was cold. Sometimes he said to a group sadly, "Oh, go away!" and after an interval angrily, "Get out of it!" at which they began to move away, looking back at him at first fearfully, then with resentment growing into hostility, and at last with laughter as they got ready to run. A stout policeman stood for a minute and observed him. The man pretended not to see, and kept his eyes upon an imaginary point in the butcher's window, until the policeman had gone away saying, "Your arm has got to go round a good many times to a pound of mutton!" The organist's eye followed the broad back to the end of the street, and remained there, fixed with helpless and subdued indignation. He only turned his head again, and that without a change of expression, when a thin woman with a quiet look of anxiety, who had stopped outside the butcher's, gave him a halfpenny. She went on down the street holding a string bag containing a cabbage close to her side: the sound of the playing had not penetrated her thoughts.

Soon after her a young clerk came along, with a pale spectacled face, dark eyes and moustache, and a look of vacant solemnity and virtue. He heard the music on his way back from the midday meal to his office, and it took entire control over his mind. He ceased to see the row of overcoats hanging up like empty skins in the office passage, the white clock and its two hands together at five minutes past one, and the head clerk looking contemptuously from him to the clock. He felt an airiness of exaltation as if he were striding over the housetops of the world in a sublime solitude. He no longer wished vaguely that he was rich, handsome, and clever, but threw his chest forward and lifted his chin complacently, while his heels struck the pavement a little more sharply and with a kind of music. He thought comfortably of several scenes in his life which be could always recall with pleasure and some glory — a cathedral full of sunlight, of spring, and of easy-walking ladies; a gorgeous banquet, a long table flashing with white and silver, glowing with fruit and flowers and wine, under many lights; a theatre, all warmth, and animation and brilliancy, just after the conclusion of a romantic first act.

These died away before a scene which he did not know. A boundless water with many islands appeared in full sunlight, such as he had never known in any August by the sea. The water sparkled in long strips and shimmered evenly in two or three broad expanses; at the edges it frothed and hissed like champagne among pebbles of many colours, of gold and turquoise and unknown gems. The islands were more luxuriant than he had ever seen or imagined. They were softly darkened at the water's edge by trees of an infinite variety of form and verdure, and illuminated by blossom in masses and sharp isolated stars. Lawns, of deep grass and of flowers in long friths of white and gold, rose and fell between the masses of trees. Such might have been the islands of the Pacific before man had touched them. Birds of gaudy plumage and arrogant shrill voices floated over the trees or hung upon the branches, and spilled the dew and the rose purple and snow of petals, in ones and twos and in woven showers, down upon the grass and the water.

The air was clear, and the light of an unearthly purity, like the air and light of imaginary lands in poems and impossible tales. There was nowhere any sign of decay or change. The sea was innocent. The sun could not set from off the islands and waters, for it hung aloft for ever in obedient majesty. All things expressed a calm and certainly immortal bliss.

What seemed at first another island floating upon the laughing water was a ship, worthy of the utmost pomp of Cleopatra. It was overgrown with flowers and leaves, so as to be known for a ship only by its motion and its high, extravagant prow and stern as it advanced slowly among the islands. While it glided, music arose; and the music seemed that of the innumerable flowers spiring up or floating down from the exuberant foliage, so soft was it and of such a nimble and thoughtless kind; and the swaying and onward rising of the vessel was beautiful of itself, as if it were wafted by the music. Birds flitted among that foliage also, and scattered without diminishing the blossoms.

With the birds, and as light and careless as they, were human beings; at least, their forms were like those made known to the young man by Titian and Correggio; and they were in harmony with the great light in the sky and upon the waters, with the flowers and the music, singing the same joy and untainted tranquillity. These were women; but high among the leaves were children, immortal children, having wings upon their shoulders. And in their wreathed motions the women and children smiled and sang melodies as sweet as if they had been, not human, but a kind of god-like birds. Their melodies joined with the mysterious singing of the vessel, and their smiles with the flowers. Some were weaving garlands and crowning or discrowning one another, and their shapes and movements were as lovely as what he dimly thought of, and imperfectly imagined, when he read: "The Graces and the rosy-bosomed Hours." Some played fantastic, musical instruments, stringed and of the form of shells and blossoms. Others were swimming close to the ship, and thrust up their smiling and golden heads through the leaves trailing upon the ripples.

These women and cherubs or cupids, the shining water, the verdure and flowers, the birds and the divine presence of the light, were pleasing to the young man beyond any of the beautiful or luxurious sights of his lifetime. They represented the utmost ease, loveliness, and exuberance, the perfection of joy and freedom, which his nature could crave. As he watched them he shed everything that had once been inconsistent with these qualities and had stood in their way. They beckoned, and their beckoning and his welcome were about to endue him with wings that he might ascend to the ship or one of the islands, that all might be accomplished according to his desire. The bliss was still far off and strange, but it was within his increasing reach, and expectation and achievement together put fire into his eyes and into his cheeks. He was no longer awkward, hurried, fatigued, ignorant, and without courage. He was the equal of those timeless creatures and a compatriot in that exquisite clime. It was as if he were made a being of divine lineage, with glorified senses, with a voice sweeter than bird, lute, or horn.

But stepping forward with blinded eagerness, he suddenly found himself stopped among the horses of the main street, in a thicket of thronging sound where the organ music was scarce audible even if sought. For some time he had not known that he was listening; now for a moment he heard it again. The vision was with him still, but in shreds and intermittently. It was more and more like a picture, having neither air nor solidity, and the horses' teeth glittered through it a grin of demons. Not only did the vision become a picture, but a picture painted upon a canvas which swayed a little in the air. The colours dimmed; the flowers were like artificial roses; the ship was impossible; the women and cupids were insipid and absurd. Yes, it was a picture he had seen somewhere — a tapestry — no, the drop-scene at a theatre, and underneath it the title "Barque d'Amour." He remembered it perfectly as he once more looked up at the office clock and its two hands together at five minutes past one.

Olwen

OLWEN was eighteen, a Welsh girl, with light brown hair so loosely coiled and so abundant that no fancy was needed to see it down to her knees; an oval face, not plump enough to conceal the bones of cheeks and bold chin; a clear, wild-rose complexion, lit up from within as by moonlight; dark eyebrows that had wild, clear curves like the wings of some bird of free waste lands, and curved lips that never hid the perfect teeth when at rest. She wore the clothes of a slattern. She walked and stood still and sat down with the pride of an animal in the first year when it has a mate. The curlew, the hare, the sheep upon the mountain, were not wilder, or swifter, or more gentle than she. Her face and stature were those of a queen in the old time, whose father was a shepherd on the solitary mountains. Being as strong as a man, she had finished her work early in the factory and come straight home, and, tucking up her skirts, had scrubbed and polished her mother's house. There was no pleasant way of being idle in the daytime, for, except with her lover, she did not care to walk to the mountain or to the black village streets. She laid tea, served it, and washed up. She was the only one who was not going out for the evening, for she had to bake the week's bread. Before the lamp had to be lit, her brother's wife came in with her baby. The first batch of cakes was already out of the oven. Their perfume streamed out through the open door, which let in the song of the blackbird, the wind from the mountains, and the majesty of evening. Olwen could rest now; she took the baby, and they sat down and began to gossip.

The married girl was a little older, slender and dark-haired, with small, sharp features and full lips, pleasure-loving, gay, and sharp-tempered, rapid in her speech. This was her first child, and she kept, as yet, all her maiden attractiveness and irresponsibility, and added to it the different power of one who is captive but unconquered. She sighed lightly now and then, as if she relished and remembered overmuch the youth she retained. She seemed to feel the advantages she had over the unmarried Olwen, without being able to overcome a phantom of admiration for her that might at any moment turn to envy.

Olwen, being the eldest of ten, held the baby like a mother. Her face bent down to it, her shoulders and arms walled it, in an experienced way. She knew all that she would ever know about the care of infants — even their death. The young mother, watching her, would now and then cull the baby from her lap and press it to herself, and cover it with kisses. If there were cries, it was Olwen who silenced them in her deep breast; but the mother had the craftiness to let the maid seem to be their cause, and when the child was with the other she would tease it, in the hope of being the comforter. It would have been hard for a stranger to say whose was the child, since Olwen's attention to this one baby out of many was as perfect as the mother's to the only one. The mother was lively and effusive, yet careless; the maid was calm and tender, and never forgetful. The mother could have been a model for Aphrodite, the maid for Demeter. The mother was a lover first; the maid was born maternal, and her heart could be stormed by a sweetheart, but ruled only by a child. The mother was destined for a man or for several men; there was somewhere a man destined for the maid, to open for her a kingdom which she would enter alone. The mother pressed the child to her with a luxurious smile, as if the lover were there, too; the maid resembled some noble animal, calm, but with a half-hid ferocity that would have talons if need were, even for the father of its brood. The mother was an elf, a not purely human creature, a haunting, disquieting form of life, a marshlight out of the wilds of time and to be blown away with time again; the maid was the beginning and the end of human life, necessity itself made beauty, mere humanity raised to a divine height, the very topmost plume on the crest of life's pride. And yet behind the physical glory of Olwen, her bold, easy gait, her deep voice, full of nobility and sweetness, behind all her courage and robustness and independence, there was a something like the timidity of the stag who stands on the rock in the moment of his greatest power and joy, without fear, and yet with an ear and a nostril for every breath of the summer gale.

  The baby was with its mother when Olwen's lover entered the room. It was still half-lit by the great fire and the pale sky after sunset. Seeing the two girls and the child, he sat in the darkest of the chairs and kept his cap in his fingers. The mother gave the child to Olwen, and the young man became silent. The maid hardly looked at him, while the young mother, glad to see a man, bantered her visitor in vain even when she said laughing:

"Olwen has a baby now, John, and you see she can do without its father."

The young man fingered his cap, but looked musingly at Olwen out of the shadow. She had no eyes or ears but for the little thing that was now fully awake and standing on her lap and putting its hands into her mouth and eyes. Now she caught it quickly under the armpits and, throwing back her head, lifted it at arm's length and let it plant its feet upon her throat, then between her breasts, and so down to her lap; it crowed and waved its limbs. The mother looked into the fire. Again Olwen stood the baby upon her head where its curled feet were entangled in her hair; her eyes were towards the young man but not looking at him, though her thoughts might have been of him. Still turned towards him, she lowered the child to her knees and jutted her bright face forward, pouting her mouth for kisses while the child tried to take away one of her glistening teeth; then she let it down flat on her knees and buried her head in the laughing and quaking form. The young man's dark eyes fixed upon her grew more and more dark and sullen, with admiration of her, jealousy of the child, and indignation that she was so careless. She had not given him a glance. She sang, she talked, she laughed, she feigned to cry, she cooed, for the child. She allowed it to do as it liked and as nobody else had done except in thought. Her cheeks glowed with pleasure and exercise and thoughts unexpressed; the white skin of her brows and throat gleamed moist and whiter than ever; her grey eyes flamed softly. Never had she been happier, and the happiness was at one with her beauty, so that a stranger watching might have thought that her happiness made her beautiful, or even that it was the consciousness of her beauty. She looked taller and her shoulders more massive than before, her back more powerful in the gentleness of its maternal stoop, her breast more deep, her dark voice more than ever the music of her noble body and blissful nature. Fit to be the bride of a hero and the mother of beautiful women and heroes and poets, she gave herself to the child.

Presently the child grew more silent, playing with a lock of her hair which now fell half over one shoulder down to her lap. She smiled musingly and caught the eye of her lover and began to tell him what she had been doing that day — how the manager had told her not to work so fast, and then asked her when she was to be married — but he remained silent. The child reared itself up by her hair and pulled at her chin and ears. She took no notice save to smile good-humouredly and shake her head, and continued to talk. Her two arms imprisoned the child; her head was raised in a pretence of keeping her chin from the enemy. Cheated of the smooth chin and soft ears the child was still a little while, and remained so still and so silent that it had been forgotten, when suddenly the mother broke into a laugh and cried:

"Well, I never, Olwen, the impudence of the child, you will be suckling her next!"

Olwen rose up undisturbed, smiling to herself, and then glancing over at John as she fastened two buttons below her neck.

"Now, Caroline," she said, "you take a turn with baby and let me talk to John."

John stood up and came forward very slowly and very stiffly, and took the child from her arms. It began at once to cry and the mother, rising in a temper, carried it swiftly away, leaving the lovers silent.

John was the first to speak, saying:

"And what did you say to the manager, Olwen? Shall we get married this summer?"

"Yes, she said; waiting is not much fun for you, John." And she gave him a kiss that he was too slow to return, so that she broke away, saying:

"And now I must take out these cakes. You light the lamp, John. Yes, come along, no nonsense. Bless me," she added, opening the oven door and letting out a smell as sweet as the first heat of May. "It's lucky I wasn't a minute later. There! Take one while it's hot and don't burn yourself. Hot cakes and maids' lips, John."

And John split the cake in two and buttered it, and they ate the halves together.

The Attempt

SEVERAL seasons had passed since Morgan Traheron had so much as looked at his fishing tackle, and now he turned over, almost indifferently, the reels and lines and hooks and flies which had been carefully put away in an old tool box of his great-grandfather's. He looked at the name "Morgan Traheron" cut neatly inside the lid, and shivered slightly during the thought that one of his own name had bought it in 1776 at the ironmonger's and brazier's under the sign of the "Anchor and Key" near Charing Cross, and that the owner had been dead nearly a hundred years. Cold, cold, must he be! Even as cold would be the younger bearer of that name, and he anticipated, in a kind of swoon, the hundred years that would one day submerge himself from all known friendliness of sun, earth, and man.

He was seeking, not any of the fishing tackle, but a revolver that lay amongst it, and a small green box containing only one ball cartridge. He had often thought of throwing the revolver away. His wife always looked wonderingly at him when he cleaned it once every year or so, but if she had urged him to throw it away he would have scoffed at the fear which he detected, all the more heartily because the sign of her concern inflated his vanity. She, lest she should provoke his mood in some way which even her consideration could not foresee, remained silent or asked him to tell again how he shot the woodpigeon fifty yards off, actually within sight of the gamekeeper's cottage. It was a thrilling and well-told tale, albeit untrue.

It was not a mere accident that one ball cartridge was left.

Morgan took out the revolver and the cartridge and shut the box. The lock was stiff and the chambers would not revolve without the use of both hands. To fire it off, it would therefore be necessary to twist the loaded chamber laboriously round to its place and then force back the hammer to full cock. The barrel was brown from rust, but probably the ball would force its way through as it had done before. It was a cheap, ugly, repulsive weapon; it impressed him with unsuitableness. He did not stay to oil it, but putting it in a pocket and the cartridge in another, he prepared to leave the house.

"Won't you take Mary with you, Morgan?" said his wife.

"Yes", said Mary, his little daughter, laughing not so much because there was anything to laugh at as because she must either laugh or cry, and certainly the chance of a walk was nothing to cry for: "Take me with you, father."

"Oh no, you don't really want to come, you only say it to please me," said Traheron, mild but hard.

"Yes, I am sure she . . . Good-bye, then," said his wife.

"Good-bye," said he.

The thought of kissing his daughter turned him back for a moment. But he did not; the act occurred to him more as part of the ceremony of this fatal day than as a farewell, and he feared to betray his thought. She was the immediate cause of his decision. He had spoken resentfully to her for some fault which he noticed chiefly because it disturbed his melancholy repose; she had then burst out crying with long, clear wails that pierced him with self-hate, remorse, regret, and bitter memory.

Why should he live who had the power to draw such a cry from that sweet mouth? So he used to ask in the luxurious self-contempt which he practised. He would delay no more. He had thought before of cutting himself off from the power to injure his child and the mother of his child. But they would suffer; also, what a rough edge would be left to his life, inevitable in any case, perhaps, but not lightly to be chosen. On the other hand, he could not believe that they would ever be more unhappy than they often were now; at least, the greater poverty which his death would probably cause could not well increase their unhappiness; and settled misery or a lower plane of happiness was surely preferable to a state of faltering hope at the edge of abysses such as he often opened for them. To leave them and not die, since the child might forget him and he would miss many a passing joy with her, was never a tolerable thought; such a plan had none of the gloss of heroism and the kind of superficial ceremoniousness which was unconsciously much to his taste. But on this day the arguments for and against a fatal act did not weigh with him. He was called to death.

He was called to death, but hardly to an act which could procure it. Death he had never feared or understood; he feared very much the pain and the fear that would awake with it. He had never in his life seen a dead human body or come in any way near death. Death was an idea tinged with poetry in his mind — a kingly thing which was once only at any man's call. After it came annihilation. To escape from the difficulty of life, from the need of deliberating on it, from the hopeless search for something that would make it possible for him to go on living like anybody else without questioning, he was eager to hide himself away in annihilation, just as, when a child, he hid himself in the folds of his mother's dress or her warm bosom, where he could shut out everything save the bright patterns floating on the gloom under his closed eyelids. There was also an element of vanity in his project; he was going to punish himself and in a manner so extreme that he was inclined to be exalted by the feeling that he was now about to convince the world he had suffered exceedingly. He had thus taken up the revolver, and blurred the moment of the report by thinking intently of the pure annihilation which he desired. The revolver was the only accessible weapon that entered his mind, and he had armed himself with it without once having performed in thought what he had committed himself to do in fact before long.

As he mounted the hill by a white path over the turf, he felt the revolver strike against his hip at each stride. He was in full view of anyone who happened to be looking out from his home, and he pressed on lest the wavering of his mind should be seen. Recalling the repulsiveness of the weapon, the idea of a rope crossed his mind, not because it was preferable, but because it was something else, something apart from his plans which now had a painful air of simplicity.

When he was among some bushes that concealed him and yet still gave him a view of his house, he paused for breath. He half-longed for an invasion of sentiment at the sight of his home; but he was looking at it like a casual stranger, and without even the pang that comes when the stranger sees a quiet house embowered in green against which its smoke rises like a prayer, and he imagines that he could be happy there as he has not until now been happy anywhere. The house was mere stones, nothing, dead. He half wished that Mary would run out into the garden and compel him to a passionate state. His will and power of action were ebbing yet lower in his lifeless mood. He moved his eyes from the house to the elder hedgerow round it, to the little woods on the undulations beyond, to the Downs, and, above them the cloudy sun perched upon a tripod of pale beams. Nothing answered his heartless call for help. He needed some tenderness to be born, a transfigured last look to keep as a memory; perhaps he still hoped that this answer that was not given to him could save him from the enemy at his side and in his brain; even so late did he continue to desire the conversion, the climacteric ecstasy by which life might solve its difficulty, and either sway placidly in harbour or set out with joy for the open sea.

He mounted the upper slopes and passed in among the beeches. He turned again, but again in vain. There was little in him left to kill when he reached the top and began to think where exactly he should go. He wished that he could hide away for ever in one of the many utterly secret mossy places known to him among beech and yew in the forsaken woods; the foxhounds might find him, but no one else. But he must go farther. The sound of the discharge must not be heard in that house below. Almost with tenderness he dreamed of the very moment when his wife would hear the news and perhaps see his body at the same time; if only that could be put off — the announcement must not come to-day, not under this sun in which the world was looking as he had always seen it, though more dull and grey, but on some day he had not known, a black, blind day yet unborn, to be still-born because of this event so important to him. Who would find him? He did not like the thought that some stranger who knew him by sight, who had never spoken to him, should come across the body, what was left of him, his remains, and should suddenly become curious and interested, perhaps slightly vain of the remarkable discovery. If only he could fade away rapidly. Several strangers with whose faces he was familiar passed him in a lane, and he assumed a proud, hard look of confidence, as he hoped.

He quickened his steps and turned into a neglected footpath where he had never met anybody. He took out the revolver and again looked at it. It was just here that he had come in the hottest of the late summer to show his daughter cinnabar caterpillars, tigerish yellow and black, among the flaming blossoms of ragwort. The ragwort was dead now, blossom and leaf. He recalled the day without comment.

He was now hidden, on one side by a dense wood, on the other by the steep slope of a hill, and before and behind by winding of the path which skirted the wood. He inserted the cartridge and with difficulty forced it into position; the brass was much tarnished. Now he revolved the chambers in order that the cartridge should be under the hammer, but by mistake turned them too far; he had to try again, and, losing count of the chambers, was again defeated. Where the cartridge was he could not be sure, and he looked to see; its tarnished disc was hostile and grim to his eye, and he hid the weapon.

Moving on, he now looked down upon a steep wood that sloped from his feet, and then rose as steeply up an opposite hill. They were beech woods with innumerable straight stems of bare branchwork that was purple in the mass. Yews stood as black islands in the woods, and they and the briers with scarlet hips close to his eye were laced with airy traveller's joy, plumy and grey.

Traheron now turned the muzzle to his temple, first letting the hammer down for fear of an accident. He had only one shot to fire, and he could not feel sure that this would enter his brain. His ear, his mouth — the thought was horrible, impossible. His skin ached with the touch of the steel which was very cold. Next he turned the weapon to his breast, and saw that he had better pull the trigger with his thumb. The hammer was now at full cock, the cartridge in place. The hideous engine looked absurdly powerful for his purpose. The noise, the wound, would be out of proportion to the little spark of life that was so willing, so eager, to be extinguished. He lowered the weapon and took a last sight of the woods, praying no prayer, thinking no thought, perfectly at ease, though a little cold from inaction.

Suddenly his eye was aware of someone moving above the opposite wood, half a mile away, and at the same moment this stranger raised a loud halloo as if he had sighted a fox, and repeated it again and again for his own delight, feeling glad, and knowing himself alone. Traheron had been watching the wood with soul more and more enchanted by the soft colour, the coldness, the repose. The cry rescued him; with shame at the thought that he might have been watched, he raised the revolver and turned it to his breast, shut his eyes and touched the trigger, but too lightly, and breathless, in the same moment, he averted the barrel and hurled it into the wood, where it struck a bough without exploding. For a moment he dreamed that he had succeeded. He saw the man who found him pick up the revolver and examine it. Finding but one cartridge in the chambers he concluded that the dead man was a person of unusual coolness and confidence, with an accurate knowledge of the position of the heart. Then, for he was cold, Traheron moved rapidly away, his mind empty of all thought except that he would go to a certain wood and then strike over the fields, following a route that would bring him home in the gentleness of evening.

He opened the door. The table was spread for tea. His wife, divining all, said:

"Shall I make tea?"

"Please," he replied, thinking himself impenetrably masked.

The Castle of Lostormellyn

THE young prince of Lostormellyn stood at a window of his castle and looked out over the world that was his. It was not yet the dawn of the autumn day, and his bride sat up in their bed and, as she mused and watched him, drew the paws of a leopard skin down over her shoulders to her breast. Turning away from the valley and its mountain boundaries and the clouds and stars, he saw that she had drawn blood with one of the talons, and asked her:

"Cariad, what is your desire?"

To which she answered:

"That the stars also were mine."

Then she hid her face in the fur, and the prince gazed out of the window again. He was waiting for the sound of his huntsman's horn to scatter the darkness and the many stars, when suddenly he poised his javelin at the sight of a strange, dark, small man looking up at him from the rocks between the tower and the abyss above which it was built.

"Before you slay me," he said quietly in the tongue of the islands of sunset, "listen to what I have come here to tell."

The prince hurled the javelin; but, nevertheless the small man having caught it and leaned forward upon it to speak, he consented to hear; and the island voice said:

"Ride to the Castle of Atheen. Ride alone, and you will have that which is most worthy of your desire."

From his bed the voice of the bride repeated the words:

"Ride to the Castle of Atheen."

The messenger had disappeared, and the prince said to himself:

"I will lead the hunt that way and will go to the Castle alone and hear what is to he heard and see what is to be seen."

He mounted his horse and all day he hunted; and the huntsmen came up with the wolf and slew it, and the prince came to the Castle of Atheen. There they poured for him the restful mead and carved the boar and gave him a bed such as was fitting for a prince and he slept well. In the morning they asked him concerning his bride and he answered them, using the words of his chief bard:

"The daughters of the mountain are the most beautiful of women, and Cariad is the most beautiful among them," and using the words of the dark messenger, added, "I have left her for a little while that I may find and bring back to her that which is most worthy of desire."

And the old queen of Atheen answered:

"I have heard of this from a dark messenger, but I am old and I did not rightly understand whereof he spoke, for it is a new thing. You must ride to the Castle of Morannog which is toward the sunset, and there they will be able to interpret the words; for the dark messenger has been a sojourner there many days."

So the young prince commanded a messenger to carry his honour and love to his bride, and mounted his horse and journeyed many days and nights over wild ways until he saw the Castle of Morannog above the mountains under the setting of the new moon. There he was entertained as a prince ought to be. He thanked them and told them wherefore he had ridden from Atheen. To which the old king and the young princes answered:

"We have a great kingdom and we are about to conquer a new, but we know not what it is that the dark messenger holds to be most worthy of desire; some say one thing and some another, and a bard has said that it is Cariad of the mountains, a very beautiful woman; but for us the next year or the next after will bring all that we have sought. Our young men are irresistible and our old men are wise."

An old man spoke also, saying:

"We have heard of the Castle of Carthinnis which lies at the borders of the West sea, and there it is said that the dark messenger is ranked with their wise men and that he has spoken familiarly with them of the things that he has learned, yes, and of the things that he has dreamed."

The young prince sent a greeting to his bride by a man of Morannog and turned the point of his spear towards Carthinnis. He rode until it seemed to him that always before him the sun was going down, and always behind him it was rising up; and beyond the sunset was the horned tower of Carthinnis. When he reached it he was glad to be at rest, to be warm, and to eat though it was but the flesh of a cormorant, and to drink though it was but water salted by the surf that blew over Carthinnis forever. He slept and dreamed that the Castle was still before him, but when he awoke nothing lay beyond save a dark sea where the moon was descending. The kingdom of the prince of Carthinnis was of rocks and of what the sea bred and cast up over them; and he had gazed so long over the sea that he cared little for speech, and he looked upon a wandering man as upon a wonderful thing that had not learned the ways of the sea. Staring at the waves between his wrinkles, he said that the dark messenger had indeed stayed with him a day or two, a year perhaps, or more — how could he say, but that it was long ago? — and all that he had learned from him was to gaze over the sea. He had spoken of ships; he had himself arrived in a ship; but who that knew so much of this sea would put forth on it? And why should a man set sail with those who fare over it when by waiting a few days he would see their faces again upon the rocks? It was from the Castle of Brintacalleg that the dark messenger came, but no man had ever spoken of it save him and he spoke of many things that for aught they knew were under the sea. Who knows if there be such a place as Brintacalleg? He led the prince down to the sea where the messenger's own ship lay still at the edge of a haven that knew the sun only upon the longest day of the year; and only once in his lifetime, said the lord of Carthinnis, had that day been clear of cloud overhead and of mist and rain between the earth and the cloud, and that was when the messenger had arrived. But the young prince sent off one of the silent men of Carthinnis with a message to his bride, and set sail for Brintacalleg, and for long, sleeping and waking under the wild sails, he saw neither the sunset before him nor the sunrise behind, except in dream. So that he knew not at last that what he saw was Brintacalleg itself, perched above the sea upon a ledge taken away from eagles, until he awoke in one of its beds and heard the singing of the maids of Brintacalleg and beheld the sun rising over the sea that he had crossed. He had already set out on foot and said farewell, when he remembered that he had not asked what they knew of the dark messenger, nor ordered that a man should take his greeting to Cariad. But he learned only that the dark messenger had served here as a scullion on his way to

Carthinnis, and that no man could take a message to Lostormellyn since the sea was impassable. "Lostormellyn?" they asked, "Lostormellyn? Is it not a Castle out of a song?" And when they had showed him the notch between the hills where the dark man had passed through on his way from the Castle of Caleeny, they said farewell and he left them and walked towards Caleeny.

When he began to walk they were reaping the barley below him, and when he reached the black walls at Caleeny, the barley was tall again in the little enclosure amidst its immeasureable woods. At Caleeny, seeing that there was but a few grey hairs in his beard, and that though on foot he was a prince, the lord offered him his youngest daughter for a bride. He told them that he was lately married to the beautiful Cariad. But as he had just told them that he had come from Brintacalleg, which was a year away to the east, nor was there such a princess there as Cariad, they smiled at this, for they knew that he had the madness of roads and the youngest daughter laughed aloud. He did not ask them the way; he had forgotten the dark messenger; but the maiden came running after him and said, with a bold smile, to his face:

"You are on the right road. Ask for Mentissat."

As he went he saw men ploughing and some sowing seed, and others mowing the hay, and others reaping. Some of them stayed to watch him go by, and some answered his questions and some did not. Only the old women going along the road at evening with faggots upon their heads wished him "Good-night."

At Mentissat, which was a white castle at the end of a long lake, they gave him to eat and drink, but because he murmured only Caleeny, Brintacalleg, Carthinnis, Morannog, Atheen, Lostormellyn, Lostormellyn, they said:

"He is from Caleeny; let us put him upon the road to Sarnollyn; for those who come to Mentissat rejoice to go forward to Sarnollyn."

Sarnollyn was a red castle among snows, and as he struggled to sleep there in the cold he dreamed of Lostormellyn and of his bride and of the dark messenger, and he awoke and questioned everyone, asking if they had seen this man. But none knew save the ancient emperor of Sarnollyn, and he replied:

"In our fathers' time such a one lived here and fed the hounds. Yet he belonged not here either, but to the Castle of Carno, which is in the desert next to the edge of the world."

The young prince muttered over the names of the Castles as he set out for the castle of Carno and remembering his bride, he paused and would have gone back to beg that a messenger should go to her and carry his honour and love, but the emperor was riding out from Sarnollyn to hunt with a thousand of his kings and their young queens and the prince was abashed and went on.

The Castle of Carno was at the extremity of a desert across many mountains that enclosed valleys as vast as a summer sky and as deep. It was not a castle at all, but a heap of stones that sheltered an old woman whose fire had gone out.

"Is this Carno?" he asked.

"It is Carno," she replied, "and beyond this is Filontry."

"Carno, Sarnollyn, Mentissat..." he was murmuring.

"Ha, ha!" laughed the old woman, "but the jest is an old one, nevertheless."

Then, the young prince said that he would go to Filontry. And as he went he did not see the roses over his head, but he saw those that had fallen to his feet.

At Filontry, which was upon a grey hill surrounded by waters, there had never been a Castle, but nevertheless in the mist the rocks had the likeness of one, and a hermit lived among them. When he saw the hermit, the young prince chanted, "Carno, Sarnollyin, Mentissat, Caleeny . . ." but the hermit waved his arm, saying:

"I know that song. I learnt it from the dark man of Colommen. Once upon a time I knew the tongue in which it is written. There was more of it, for it ended Larmontandro, Colonagry, Colommen. They say that Larmontandro is the name of a Castle like this — over there — but I have never seen it. You are used to the road: go then and discover Larmontandro and bring me word."

When the young prince came to Larmontandro, there was a bird that sang the name, "Larmontandro," upon a withered oak that was one of three in a valley running from there down to the sea, and at its end there was a pile of rocks like a castle above the sea. The mountain side was too steep, so he followed the valley towards the rocks.

On his way he passed a well that bubbled and seemed to say "Colonagry, Colonagry," and as he walked he kept time to his steps with the song, "Colonagry, Larmontandro, Filontry, Carno, Sarnollyn, Mentissat, Caleeny, Brintacalleg, Carthinnis, Morannog, Atheen, and Lostormellyn, Colommen," and he said: "I have learned a jest and a song."

The nearer he approached to the sea the more like a castle was that pile of rocks, but a castle so huge that it could not have been raised by hands. As the road wound he thought, "It is the Castle of Brintacalleg": and again, "It is Atheen"; and not once only he thought, "Lostormellyn was like this if I both see and remember right." The farther he went the more like was it to Lostormellyn, except that Lostormellyn was not by the sea. The road wound far under the walls, and he thought that Cariad was looking out of a window and looking for him and he shouted, but it was too high. He quickened his pace and climbed round and round the rocks until he was before the gate which was like that of Lostormellyn as a poplar tree is like the flower of the grass.

He struck upon the door and it was opened by the dark messenger who greeted him with a smile of welcome but not of recognition, saying only:

"You have come, O prince, to what is most worthy of desire."

"Lead me," said the prince, "to Cariad."

"Yes, to Cariad," said the dark man as they mounted the stairs, "Cariad is queen."

At last they came to a great room like his own, and at the window he saw Cariad and the back of her beautiful head was towards him. He tried to speak, but he could not, and still she did not turn. He thought that she dreamed, and when he reached the bed, because he was weary, he lay down upon it and drew the leopard skin over his shoulders. Then she bent her eyes full of love upon him and said: "Lostormellyn is fair tonight and it is as if the stars also were ours between this and the mountains. Sweetest after hunting is rest with the beloved. This hour is most worthy of desire."

But the young prince had begun to say over the names of the Castles upon the road, and suddenly exclaimed:

"But Colommen? Where is Colommen? I did not go to Colommen."

"It is," said Cariad, "it is the name I bore when I was among the mountains before you carried me down to Lostormellyn."

"You know not what you say," he said, repeating the name.

"It is the name also," said Cariad, "of a city in a song."

"In a song!" he cried. "That is what they said of Lostormellyn when I was at Brintacalleg."

"And so it is," she mused aloud: "for there are many songs."

"Are you then," he murmured half to himself, "are you then a woman in a song or Cariad? They will tell me you are in a song some day."

Then he leaped up to clasp her. But she was gone without a sign, and he cried:

"It is a dream. It is a song."

The dark messenger at his side also said;

"It is a dream. It is worthy of a man's desire."

The horns of morning sounded round Lostormellyn, but could not waken the prince.